Here's what teens are saying about Bluford High:

"As soon as I finished one book, I couldn't wait to start the next one. No books have ever made me do that before."
—*Terrance W.*

"The suspense got to be so great I could feel the blood pounding in my ears."
—*Yolanda E.*

"Once I started reading them, I just couldn't stop, not even to go to sleep."
—*Brian M.*

"Great books! I hope they write more."
—*Eric J.*

"When I finished these books, I went back to the beginning and read them all over again. That's how much I loved them."
—*Caren B.*

"I found it very easy to lose myself in these books. They kept my interest from beginning to end and were always realistic. The characters are vivid, and the endings left me in eager anticipation of the next book."
—*Keziah J.*

BLUFORD HIGH

Secrets in the Shadows

ANNE SCHRAFF

Series Editor: Paul Langan

SCHOLASTIC INC.

New York Toronto London Auckland Sydney
Mexico City New Delhi Hong Kong Buenos Aires

ISBN-13: 978-0-439-90485-8
ISBN-10: 0-439-90485-4

12 11 10 9 8 7 6 5   8 9 10 11 12/0

Printed in the U.S.A.   01

First Scholastic printing, January 2007

Chapter 1

Roylin Bailey flipped on the bathroom switch and yelled, "Mom, the switch still don't work! Didn't Tuttle fix it yet? This dump is falling apart!"

"Roylin, that man don't do nothin' around here. All he wants is to go to that racetrack and bet on horses. He'd keep gamblin' even if the ceiling fell down on us! Yesterday I had to wash the baby in water I heated on the stove 'cause we don't have enough hot water to fill a teacup!" Mrs. Bailey called back. She had complained many times, but Tuttle, the building manager, was a sour-tempered little man who always had several days' stubble on his face and a greasy Dodgers cap on his head. Requests from the tenants fell on deaf ears. But with five children, Mrs. Bailey had few choices of where to live in this neighborhood.

Roylin was almost seventeen, and he had a pretty good job as a waiter at the Golden Grill restaurant. He worked three days a week and could bring home decent money in tips, especially on Saturday nights. But most of his earnings went to pay for insurance on his mother's Honda. Because he paid for the insurance, his mother allowed him to drive the car to work and school. Between gas, insurance, and clothes, there was no way Roylin could afford to help his mother pay for a better place to live.

"Man, this place ain't fit for the roaches on the walls," Roylin yelled, kicking the bathroom door shut.

"Don't take it out on us," said Amberlynn, Roylin's fourteen-year-old sister.

"Shut your mouth!" he snapped from behind the closed door.

"Don't talk to me like that," Amberlynn yelled back. "I need a ride to school this morning," she added. "Can you take me?"

"No!"

"Mom, Roylin won't drive me to school!" Amberlynn whined.

"It's outta my way. Take the bus or walk," Roylin snapped, stepping out of the bathroom.

"What's your problem?" Amberlynn said. "You're just like Dad—mean and ugly."

Roylin turned sharply and glared at his sister. "Don't you *ever* say I'm like him! You hear me? I'm nothin' like him, nothin'!" Roylin's father used to beat him regularly, using a heavy leather strap to turn Roylin's back into a mass of tender bruises. The slightest offense was enough to enrage the muscular man. He would stand Roylin against the wall and administer blow after blow. That was why Roylin's mother finally divorced him. Even being alone with five children was not as frightening to her as living with a man whose wrath was dangerous and unpredictable. Nobody ever knew whose turn it would be to be beaten. Would he use the strap on Roylin, would he crack Amberlynn across her face, splitting her lip, or would he shove his wife so hard against the sink that she would ache for days?

"Drive your sister," Mom said crossly. "You can do that much, Roylin Bailey. It's startin' to rain, and it's a long walk to the middle school, and the bus is runnin' late as usual."

Roylin hiked his backpack onto his

shoulders. "Hurry up if you're comin' with me, Amberlynn. I don't wanna be late for my first class and get locked out."

Amberlynn stuffed one more book into her backpack and ran after her brother as he headed for his Honda. Once inside the car, Amberlynn said, "I made it onto the cheerleading squad, me and Jamee Wills. Granelli's Paint Store is paying for the uniforms. They're so nice! I'll be so good at cheering that when I get to Bluford next year I can be on the cheerleading squad there."

"Like I care," Roylin muttered.

"Hey, ain't that Bobby Wallace, that wannabe thug who was hangin' out with Londell James when you got shot?" Amberlynn asked. "How come he ain't in jail or something?"

"That punk copped a plea, and now he's back in school. They got Londell for that drive-by, though. He's the one who pulled the trigger," Roylin said, remembering the day in the park when he was shot. The memory of it still made him tremble.

Roylin pulled up at the middle school and said, "Get goin', girl. I gotta make it to Bluford before the first bell, or it's my neck. Eckerly is the meanest teacher in Bluford, and she'd just love to mess me up."

Amberlynn rushed out of the car, and Roylin drove on to Bluford High School. Steering the teal-blue Honda through the morning drizzle, he pulled into the parking lot, bolted from the car, and sprinted into the school, careful to avoid the shallow puddles that had formed on the cracked asphalt.

"Hey man," Cooper Hodden laughed as Roylin skidded into the classroom, "you always tryin' to get in under the wire. Why don't you just get up a little earlier, man?"

Roylin ignored the comment. He was sitting down when he saw a new girl sitting a desk away. She was the most beautiful girl Roylin had ever seen, even in his dreams. Her skin looked like satin, and she had huge dark eyes shadowed by long lashes. Her slightly pouting lips were smooth, full, and red.

"Man," Roylin whistled softly, "who is *that?*"

Tarah Carson sat behind Roylin. "Fool," she whispered to Roylin, "don't even *think* about that girl. Her name is Korie Archer, and she thinks she is *all that!*"

Roylin paid no attention to Ms. Eckerly's lecture on Civil War battles. He kept staring at Korie, at the way she tilted her head when she was puzzled, at how her smooth hand rubbed her neck when she grew tired of looking at the chalkboard. Roylin had dated other girls, and some of them were pretty, but no girl he had ever seen measured up to Korie. She was somebody he expected to see on the cover of a magazine, not sitting in his classroom. She had one of those incredible faces and bodies that do not seem to belong in the real world, especially the world Roylin Bailey lived in.

Roylin watched Korie glide from the room when class ended. Her perfect figure swayed through the crowd of students in the hallway. He jostled past several others to catch up to her. "Hi," he said nervously. "I'm Roylin Bailey. Today's your first day here, huh?"

Korie turned and flashed a big smile. "Yeah, I'm Korie Archer. I'm a transfer from Hoover. Do you like it here?"

"Yeah, I mean, it's okay. I'll show you around. What's your next class?"

Korie hesitated for a minute and then dug in her overcrowded purse. "I don't even know. I am so confused . . . Let's see, where's my schedule?" A lipstick and small compact fell from her purse as she rummaged around, and Roylin dove to the floor to recover them for her. When Roylin returned them, her hand brushed his, and electricity seemed to pulsate through his body. "Oh, here's the schedule. I got science next."

"I'll show you where it is," Roylin volunteered as they walked on.

"Thanks," Korie said in a musical, breathy voice.

"You got biology with Reed. She's tough. There's Room 112, right there." Roylin pointed to an open door with students streaming in.

"Well, thanks a lot, Roylin. You've been really sweet," Korie said, smiling. How could Tarah have said Korie thought she was hot stuff? She seemed as nice as she was beautiful.

"Uh . . . Korie, you and I are both in the same lunch period," Roylin said, studying her schedule carefully. "I can meet you after your algebra class, and we can go to lunch together, okay? If the rain stops, we can even go outside and eat under the trees."

"Oh, that'd be great 'cause I don't know anybody here, and I hate eating alone. You're a really nice guy, Roylin. I'm so glad I ran into you," Korie said.

"I'll meet you outside your class-room, and we'll go over to the cafeteria together," Roylin babbled on, his words tumbling over one another. "And I'll show you what's good to eat, too, 'cause some of the food here is nasty."

"Thanks," Korie said, as she headed toward class. She paused at the door and gave Roylin a little wave before dis-appearing into the lab classroom.

This can't be real, Roylin thought. He must be asleep in his run-down apart-ment having an incredible dream about a fantasy girl who actually treated him like a winner instead of the loser he really was. A guy like Hakeem Randall who could sing and play the guitar—who could make students cheer because they liked and respected him—that is the kind of guy a girl like Korie would date. Nice, pretty girls like Korie never had anything to do with the Roylins of the world. Roylin was the kind of guy girls made fun of when they gossiped about boys.

Sure, it was partly his own fault. Sometimes he taunted kids so they would feel as bad as he did. He was often rude too, but he never wanted to hurt people the way his father did. He remembered hating how his father acted, and yet he often found himself doing the same kinds of things, like he was following a script his father had written for him. Sometimes he felt trapped inside his own skin. But recently things seemed to be changing.

Since the day Roylin was grazed by a bullet at Tarah's party, people had been treating him differently. Several times over the past month, Cooper Hodden threw an arm around Roylin's shoulders and called him, "Roylin, my man." Even Hakeem invited him to join the Bluford Park Crew, a group of students who worked to keep a nearby park free from beer bottles, graffiti, and trash.

It was hard to be mean when everyone was being so nice, but Roylin knew better than to trust what was happening. He figured Cooper and Hakeem felt sorry for him, that being nice to him was just a form of charity.

But Korie was different. If she liked him, maybe things really would change. Roylin felt as if his morning classes would never end. All he could think about was having lunch with Korie.

When the bell finally rang, Roylin leaped from his desk and raced to the lab classroom so he could meet Korie.

"Hey, Roylin," Hakeem called. "Wanna study algebra with me at lunch? The quiz is coming up, and you said you wanted to work together."

"No, not today. I'm busy, real busy," Roylin said, rushing past Hakeem. As he neared the science room, he noticed Korie had already come out and was talking to Steve Morris, a varsity running back for the Bluford Buccaneers.

"No, no, no," Roylin muttered to himself, "get away from her, man. I'll bust your head! I seen her first. Don't you move in on her now!"

Roylin came up to Korie, turned his back to Steve, and said, "Let's go, Korie. We want to get in the front of the line at the cafeteria."

"Hi, Roylin. Steve was just telling me about the Bluford Buccaneers and how good you guys were this year . . ." Korie said.

"I played with the Buccaneers too," Roylin said, omitting the fact that he was a mediocre player who quit so he could work more hours. "Come on, Korie. Let's go."

"'Bye, Steve," Korie sang out as she

fell in step beside Roylin. "Everybody is so nice here. I love Bluford already, and this is only my first day!"

Roylin cast a nervous glance at the girl who, miraculously, was walking with *him.* The vultures were circling. Guys like Steve were ready to pounce on every pretty girl. But not Korie, Roylin thought. Korie belonged to him.

Chapter 2

At lunchtime, Roylin managed to get to the front of the line with Korie. "The pizza is really good here, Korie. And the chocolate cake," Roylin explained.

"No, I'll get fat if I eat all that. I think I'll stick with salad," Korie said.

The sun had come out, and Roylin and Korie took their trays to a corner bench outside under some old oak trees. "I got a car, you know, Korie, a nice Honda. I got a job too, down at the Golden Grill, and they really like me down there. Some of the customers come in and ask for me 'cause I know how to treat people."

"Wow," Korie said, smiling and looking into Roylin's eyes, "most guys our age don't have money . . . I mean, you're lucky if they buy you a bag of fries!"

"Not me. I got plenty of money," Roylin lied. He was struggling this month just to pay for his car insurance. But Roylin wanted desperately to impress Korie.

"You know," Korie said, carefully stabbing her fork into a juicy slice of tomato, "my birthday is coming up in two weeks. I'm gonna be sweet sixteen."

"I'm turnin' seventeen," Roylin said.

"Well, we'll have to celebrate each other's birthdays, huh, Roylin?"

"Yeah, you bet. I'm the one in the family makin' the most money, so I buy most of the gifts. My sister, she's younger than me, and all she wants is sweaters and maybe some sparkly thing, like a bracelet or something," Roylin said. "Do you like jewelry?"

"Ohhh, it's my weakness. I saw a necklace in this little jewelry store the other day, and I am dying for it! But my parents will probably get me some stupid pair of pajamas or a bathrobe or something. I mean, money is tight around our house, but still, what kind of birthday gift is a pair of pajamas?" Korie smiled at Roylin and searched through her purse for something. "But I shouldn't be bothering you with my troubles," she said, pulling out a small mirror.

"No, I want you to share stuff with me. Know what, Korie, I could drive you home after school. Maybe we could stop at that jewelry store, and you could show me that necklace. I mean, it'd be fun for me to see what kind of things you like, you know . . ."

"Ohhh, Roylin, it is *so* beautiful. I mean, you would not believe how beautiful it is. I'm telling you, it's just the most incredible necklace I ever saw, Roylin," Korie said, delight on her face.

During study hall that afternoon, Roylin figured out his budget on a pad of paper. He had six hundred dollars, and his car insurance payment would take all but fifty bucks. That was how much he could spend on Korie's birthday gift. Roylin bought sparkly little pins for his mother for under five dollars. It would be no problem to get the necklace for fifty, but if it was more, maybe Roylin could borrow some money from his mother. Or maybe he could get it from old Ambrose Miller, who lived in the same apartment building as the Baileys. Roylin and Mr. Miller went way back. As a boy, Roylin looked at Mr. Miller as the closest thing he ever had to a grandfather, somebody who really cared about him. From time to time Mr. Miller slipped Roylin money, even a twenty-dollar bill for doing chores.

Roylin's brain was spinning. If he got that necklace for Korie, she would almost belong to him, he thought. It would not matter how many better-looking, smoother guys came along to hit on her. She would owe it to Roylin to be his girl.

Suddenly a sick and painful memory rushed into Roylin's mind, sneaking up on his thoughts like a mugger. Dad always talked about 'owning' people. He would stand in the kitchen screaming at Mom, *"You're my woman, you hear me? You're mine. As long as I'm the one out there bustin' my butt to keep food on the table, I'm makin' the rules. And you'll do what I say."* He would grab Mom by the arm and shake her real hard. For days afterwards, Mom would be careful not to wear short sleeves because she was ashamed of the dark bruises.

Roylin felt sick as he sat at his desk. He never planned to treat people like Dad treated Mom and the kids. A few times Roylin shoved Amberlynn in anger, and once he even spanked the boys, but he made up his mind right then that he would not do that again. He did not want to be like his father. He hated that man so much he could taste it, the way you taste onions long after you have had them.

After school, Roylin took Korie to his car. "Oh, what a nice car," Korie said. "Our car is some ratty old van. I am so embarrassed to be seen in it."

As Roylin drove from the school parking lot, he saw Hakeem, Darcy, and some other Bluford kids watching him. He imagined they were all probably racking their brains right now trying to figure out how Roylin Bailey, the loser, got the most beautiful girl at Bluford to ride in his car. *Look at me now*, Roylin thought. He grinned and waved proudly.

"Where's the jewelry store, Korie?" he asked.

"It's in the mall. I can't wait until you see this necklace. It's fit for a princess. Someday I'm going to have it!" Korie sighed.

"You *are* a princess," Roylin said.

Roylin could not believe how nice it was to be out with Korie. In the parking lot as they headed toward the mall entrance, he nervously reached for her hand, and she gave it to him with a playful smile, as if they had been going out for months. He felt so proud with Korie at his side.

On the way to the jewelry store,

Roylin could feel the looks of passing guys, the envious stares. Korie was the kind of girl who *always* got attention, and the guys were obviously wondering what an average-looking dude like him was doing with a girl like her.

As they walked into the jewelry store, Roylin felt very awkward. They were the only teenagers in the store. An older woman glared at them the second they stepped onto the store's plush carpet. *"What are you doing here?"* her expression seemed to say.

Before Roylin could say anything, Korie led him by the hand to a glass case at the back of the store. "There it is," she cried, pointing to a gold necklace shimmering with tiny diamonds. "Isn't it amazing?"

Roylin peered into the display and noticed a small blood-red ruby at the bottom of the necklace. The price tag was on a card leaning against the box. Two hundred and ninety-nine dollars!

Roylin felt as if he had been hit in the stomach by the heavyweight champion of the world.

"Is that beautiful or *what*?" Korie exclaimed.

Roylin heard himself chattering, saying stupid things like, "Don't be surprised if you get the necklace for your birthday, Korie." It was like his mouth was not connected to his brain anymore. Where was he going to get three hundred dollars?

"Roylin!" Korie cried. "We hardly know each other. Don't be silly! I mean, I didn't bring you to look at the necklace so *you* would buy it for me!" But Korie was smiling and giggling as if that was just what was on her mind.

Roylin realized he had stupidly bragged about all the money he had. Korie probably figured he could easily afford the necklace. She was laughing so hard with delight that she tumbled into Roylin's arms. When he put his hand on her back, she snuggled as if she really liked him holding her. Then, still smiling, Korie pulled away and gasped, "Oh, look at us! Aren't we terrible? People are gawking and thinking, 'Look at those kids!' Oh, look at that old lady staring at us! I bet she's thinking, 'What is the world coming to?' I bet she goes home and says to all the other old ladies, 'Oh my word, the kids today are just *awwww-ful*. You should have seen them carryin' on in the mall. They don't care what they do in public!'" Korie had changed her voice to mimic old age, and Roylin thought it was

18

the funniest thing he ever heard and started laughing too.

"Let's give her a real show," he said, grabbing Korie and kissing her, as if it were part of the game they were playing and not something he had desperately wanted to do since he first saw her. Korie agreeably wrapped her arms around Roylin's neck and kissed him back. They stumbled apart then, laughing and nearly delirious from excitement. He had kissed Korie. His heart pounded so hard and fast, he thought he might die at any moment, and he did not care.

As they walked back to the parking lot, Korie said, "Now Roylin, I don't want you to even *think* about buying that necklace for me. I would feel terrible if you spent all that money."

"I got a lot of money, Korie," Roylin lied. "I mean, I'm always getting expensive jewelry for my Mom. What good is money if you can't spend it on making people happy?" Roylin knew the truth was that his mother was lucky if he bought her a seven-dollar box of candy for her birthday, or maybe a cheap piece of costume jewelry.

"Roylin, you are something else!" Korie exclaimed.

After dropping Korie off at her apartment, in a building as dismal as the one he lived in, Roylin rushed home. He needed to lay his hands on two hundred and fifty dollars really quick. He had all but promised to buy that necklace for Korie, and if he went back on his promise, he would be a liar in her eyes. He could not bear to even imagine that.

"Mom," Roylin said, finding his mother in the kitchen, "I need a loan. I'll pay you back and everything, but—"

"A loan? How much?" Mom asked, checking on the macaroni casserole.

"Uh . . . like two hundred and something," Roylin said.

Mom turned, her hands pressed to her cheeks. "Oh my Lord! You're in trouble, aren't you, boy? You owe money to some thugs, don't you? Oh merciful Lord, what happened?"

"Mom! Nothin' like that. Everything is going real great, Mom. But, see, I met this real classy girl, and I need to get her something real nice for her birthday, and she's got her heart set on this necklace . . ." Roylin blurted it out before realizing what a mistake that was. All his life, his mother pinched pennies and clipped coupons, and he dared talk about spending hundreds on a girl-friend.

"Roylin Bailey, get outta here!" Mom yelled. "Have you lost your mind? You want to spend all that money on some little high school girl? You must be crazy! How can you ask such a thing? I can feed this family for a month on that!"

"Okay, okay, forget it," Roylin snapped. "I shoulda known you wouldn't under-stand. You don't understand nothin'!"

Amberlynn, who had been listening from the doorway, said, "Roylin, you never talked about having a girlfriend. You musta just met her."

"That makes it even worse," Mom ranted on. "You want to give an expen-sive gift to a girl you don't even know! Roylin Bailey, sometimes I believe you done lost the sense God gave you!"

Roylin glared at Amberlynn. "Why don't you stay out of it! No one asked for your opinion, stupid."

Amberlynn folded her arms defiantly and said, "You can call me all the names you want, but you don't scare me no more. You're just a wannabe, and that's why you have to bribe some girl into dat-ing you, 'cause she never would want you otherwise!"

21

Roylin stormed out of the house and jumped into his Honda. Maybe he could get some money from someone at school. He found Hakeem and Cooper hanging out at Niko's, the local pizza place.

"Okay," Roylin said, "who wants to make me a loan? I can pay the money back in two months with interest."

Cooper looked at Hakeem. "Do we look like bankers?" he asked.

Hakeem smiled and turned to Roylin. "How much we talking about, man?"

"Two hundred fifty," Roylin said.

"Two hundred fifty!" Cooper howled. "You musta got hit on the head with a football, and it messed up your brains to think we got that kind of change."

"What're you needing that kind of money so fast for, anyway?" Hakeem asked. "You must be pulling down at least a couple hundred a month at the Golden Grill, aren't you?"

"Yeah, but the car payments and the insurance is killin' me," Roylin said. "It's eatin' me up and I need cash *bad.*"

"If we were talkin' five bucks or something, I'd give it to you in a minute, man," Cooper said.

"I could give you ten maybe, but that's a strain," Hakeem said.

"I don't need no chump change!" Roylin snapped, stomping out of the pizza place.

What am I gonna do? Roylin asked himself as he ran back to his car. He had to get the money for Korie's necklace—he *had* to.

Chapter 3

Guys in the neighborhood made easy money selling dope, but Roylin knew which direction that street was going—straight down. He never wanted to be the one standing before the judge, wearing steel bracelets. Roylin's father did time twice, and each time he came out meaner and more useless than before. Roylin wanted no part of that. There was only one way to get the money he needed—he had to ask his neighbor, Ambrose Miller.

Mr. Miller surely had the money. Roylin knew his leather wallet was always stuffed with cash. And he never went anywhere to spend his money. On most days, he sat in his worn, overstuffed chair watching TV and nibbling on cookies. He explained many times why he refused to keep his money in a bank.

"When I was young, them banks all went belly up, and no one could get their money. If that ever happens again, I'm gonna to be okay, and you will too, boy. I'll make sure of that," he once told Roylin.

When Roylin was small, he and Mr. Miller were very close. Mr. Miller had a collection of tiny race cars, and he would always bring them out so Roylin could play. As a boy, Roylin spent many afternoons pushing the cars through the little living room and hallway in Mr. Miller's apartment. Since he started working, Roylin did not visit the old man as much, but he knew if there was anyone he could turn to in a tight spot, it was Mr. Miller.

Roylin returned to his apartment, wondering how he would explain things to his old friend. He had never asked Mr. Miller for anything, and he felt strange doing it now. In recent weeks, Tuttle, the building manager, had complained about how Mr. Miller was going senile and that he did not take care of his apartment. Once Tuttle even threatened to send a letter to Mr. Miller's out-of-state daughter saying that the old man should be put into a nursing home. But no matter what Tuttle said, Mr. Miller always seemed fine to Roylin. He was sure that if he told Mr. Miller about Korie, his old friend would try to help him.

Roylin walked down the long hallway towards Mr. Miller's apartment. He was startled by Tuttle, who was emptying trash nearby. He cackled when he saw Roylin stop at Mr. Miller's door. "What're you going in there for? He got no sense, old as he is. He just sits in the chair. I think he's demented. Wonder why he don't die. What good is a demented old man like him, anyway?" Tuttle moved on then, still cackling, and dragging a large bag of trash behind him.

Roylin knocked gently on Mr. Miller's door. The old door slowly creaked open. Roylin could see Mr. Miller asleep in his chair. The TV was blaring loudly.

"Mr. Miller," Roylin said as he came into the room, but the old man slept on, snoring with an occasional burst of sound that shook his frail body.

Roylin glanced at the end table and saw the wallet by the lamp. There it sat, bulging with money that Roylin so desperately needed. If Mr. Miller were awake, he would surely want to help Roylin out. What good was the money to him anyway?

Shaking, Roylin picked up the fat wallet. He drew out some bills—fifties, twenties, tens. Roylin began to count them out. He took two fifties, five twenties and five tens. There was more in the wallet, but he did not take any more.

"I'll pay you back, Mr. Miller," he whispered. *It's not really stealing*, Roylin thought as he took the money, *just borrowing from a friend.* And yet as he turned to leave Mr. Miller's apartment, Roylin was deeply ashamed. Only the image of Korie flooding through his mind could have made him do this.

Shoving the money deep into his pocket, Roylin rushed from the apartment, nearly colliding with Tuttle, who was mopping the hallway.

"Boy, watch your step," the little man growled as Roylin raced past him.

Roylin ignored Tuttle's comment and sprinted out to his Honda. He had to purchase the gold necklace before someone else did. All he could think of was placing the sparkling chain on Korie's neck and hearing her scream with joy when he gave it to her.

Once in the mall, Roylin dashed into the jewelry store and bought the necklace

27

with fifty dollars of his own money and the two hundred and fifty from Mr. Miller's wallet.

"Well, you are certainly going to make somebody happy," the salesclerk said cheerfully. "I bet you worked long and hard for the money."

Roylin had been smiling, but now his smile faded. Why did the clerk say that? Was it sarcasm? Did she suspect something? Roylin snatched up the box and hurried from the store. He felt entirely different than he had ever felt in his life. As he left the mall, he felt certain that people were watching him, judging him.

Korie's birthday was on a Friday, and Roylin thought he would ask her out to dinner. He would wait until they finished eating, and then he would hand her the box. She would know right away what was in it. And she would be so grateful to Roylin that she would want to be his girlfriend forever.

Roylin parked his Honda and headed for the apartment, the small necklace box hidden in his jacket pocket. He hoped no one in his family would ask him what he was doing all evening. He was too excited and nervous to face anybody just now.

Roylin was in luck. His mother had gone to bed early after a long day of work, and his sister did not seem to notice him creep into the bedroom. Quickly he hid the tiny box under his mattress, undressed, and got into bed. As long as everyone thought he was asleep, no one would ask him what he had done since school ended. For hours, Roylin tossed and turned in his bed. Taking that money from Mr. Miller kept haunting him, no matter how hard he tried to forget it. Mr. Miller had always been his friend, his best friend, his *only* friend.

The next morning, Roylin did not say much at breakfast. He kept thinking how thrilled Korie would be when she got her gift. And he kept wondering if Mr. Miller missed his money yet. As Roylin hurried from the apartment to go to school, he tried not to look at Mr. Miller's door with its chipped paint. Roylin consoled himself with thinking about how he would return the money. The minute he got paid, he would slip a couple of tens into Mr. Miller's wallet. Lately the old man was often confused. He would just think he had mislaid the money. Then, little by

29

little, Roylin would pay it all back. Then he would not be a thief anymore.

All day at school, two emotions kept clashing in Roylin's head. He was full of excitement about the wonderful moments with Korie that lay ahead of him, and he was nagged by guilt over taking money from Mr. Miller. Roylin had often daydreamed in class, but today each hour passed by in a blur because he was lost in his own private world.

The only time Roylin was able to focus was when he was with Korie. In history class she sat next to him, and they scribbled little notes back and forth to each other. Roylin had so much fun he nearly forgot he was in class, until Ms. Eckerly warned them. "I hope you two have as much to write in your history reports as you do to each other," she said. A few kids in the class chuckled. Roylin did not worry. He had done most of his report already during a slow night at work. It did not matter anyway, he thought. He never got above a C on anything, no matter how hard he worked.

Later that day, Roylin met Korie for lunch. He had to keep himself from telling her about the present he had gotten her.

"So what are you getting me for my birthday?" Korie asked playfully, smiling at him as he took a bite of pizza. Roylin could feel his heart flutter. He still could not believe how attractive she was and how great she treated him compared to the other girls at Bluford.

"I might have gotten a little something for you," he said, trying to act calm. "But you're gonna have to wait." Roylin could barely stop himself from running home, getting the necklace, and giving it to her right then. He knew that once he gave it to her, he would have the girl of his dreams.

"Roylin, I can't believe you're teasing me like this," Korie said, folding her arms across her chest. "Can't you even give me a little hint?" She formed her lips into a perfect pout.

"I'll say this," Roylin began, full of pride, "once you see it, you're gonna wanna be my girl forever."

A smile spread across Korie's face. "Oooh," she cooed. "I can't wait!"

As soon as lunch ended and Korie left, Roylin's day again faded into a thick fog. The longer he was away from her, the more he became lost in his thoughts of Mr. Miller. He could not wait to get home and talk to the old man to see if he missed his money. If he did not even notice it was gone, then the pressure to return it quickly would be off Roylin. But if Mr. Miller was really upset about the missing money, Roylin might even tell him the truth right away. At least then, Roylin thought, he would be honest with his old friend.

Coming home that afternoon, Roylin noticed Tuttle standing on the sidewalk.

"I been waitin' for you, boy."

"You want to talk to me about repairing the busted light in the bathroom or about us having no hot water?" Roylin snapped.

"Something a little more serious than that," Tuttle said, squinting his beady eyes. He blinked rapidly, and his sandpapery voice was low, as if he had something horrible to say. "Poor Mr. Miller died last night," he said.

"Mr. Miller *died?!*" Roylin gasped. "But . . ." He was about to say he saw him last evening and he seemed fine, sleeping in his chair before the television. But Roylin thought better of saying that.

"Yes, he died. Poor old wretch had a heart attack. It was the shock that killed him. I'm sure of that," Tuttle said, pausing for his words to have the desired effect. "The theft, you know."

"I don't know what you're talkin' about," Roylin cried, but a volcano of grief and guilt exploded within him.

"He woke up and found the money missin' from his wallet . . . and then he had the fatal seizure . . . so in a way, Roylin, you are guilty of murder. You see, if you are committin' a crime against someone, and they die as a result, well, that's murder," Tuttle said.

"You're crazy," Roylin stammered. "I never took no money. What're you talkin' about?"

"I saw you, boy. I saw you sneak into his room and fiddle with his wallet last night. I saw you come out and run like a thief. I didn't think you took more than a couple of dollars, so I didn't say anything. But when the poor old fool cried out to me and said a *lot* of money was gone . . . he was clutchin' at his chest and flailin' on the floor. I could tell he was a goner. I would have called for help, but I knew he was dead. I used to work in a mortuary, and I know what death looks like," Tuttle said, seeming to enjoy the look of growing torment on Roylin's face. "Now, I don't think we need to involve the police, do you? Miller was real old, and his time would have come pretty quickly anyway, so this is what I'd like to do—we won't say anything to anyone, just let on that he moved somewhere else. With your help, I can get the body downstairs once it gets dark . . . bury him down there and let it be the end of it."

"You're crazy," Roylin gasped.

"Watch your mouth, boy. *I saw what you did.* Don't you *ever* forget that. Only reason I'm willin' to cover this up is I'm gettin' too old for all these chores around the building, and I'm expectin' that out of gratitude for how I helped you hide your crime, you'll be helpin' me around the place. So, take your choice. Do things my way, or we'll just call the police right now and tell them what happened. What do you say, boy?"

"I don't want nothin' to do with this," Roylin cried, backing away from Tuttle. "I ain't buryin' no body!"

"Then I'll just call the police. Oh, by the way, I carefully slipped Mr. Miller's wallet into a plastic bag to preserve your

34

fingerprints. You in big trouble, boy."
Tuttle's cackling laughter grew more
sinister. He reached up with his grimy
fingers and adjusted his greasy baseball
cap.

Roylin closed his eyes as waves of
terror washed over him. His father had
talked a lot about life in prison, the horror of it. Roylin could not face being
arrested, spending years in prison, having his whole future destroyed.

"Okay," Roylin whispered, "what do
you want me to do?"

Chapter 4

"Just help me carry the . . . remains down to the basement. The cement floor is thin in places. I'll break through it and bury old Mr. Miller underneath the building," Tuttle said.

"Stop talkin' about it!" Roylin cried.

Tuttle continued in a soft monotone, "We'll tell the other tenants that Mr. Miller got sick and was taken off to a nursing home. I've been talking about that anyway, and some of Miller's old friends here know his daughter was planning to put him away. Nobody need be the wiser. I'll handle the social security checks that the postman leaves. We'll say Mr. Miller is much better off where he is," Tuttle added, his lips twisting into a thin, menacing smile.

Roylin followed Tuttle to Mr. Miller's door. As they stepped into the apartment,

Roylin started to tremble. What would Mr. Miller's body look like? Would his eyes be open? Roylin knew that if he looked at Mr. Miller's poor dead face, he would have that awful image imprinted in his mind forever. But when Roylin came into the familiar room, the body was already securely wrapped in a blanket and bound with twine. Mr. Miller's remains looked like nothing so much as a mummy.

"Think of it as just a heavy object, and it'll be easier to handle," Tuttle advised as they picked it up. Roylin and Tuttle carried the body down the back stairs to Tuttle's basement apartment.

Smells of stale cigarette smoke and garbage filled the basement. It was dirty and unkempt, like a rat's nest. It seemed a perfect home for Tuttle. Roylin felt as if he were going to be sick.

"Here we go," Tuttle said as they put the body down. "I'll bury him. It may take some time, but don't worry about it. Old Tuttle will handle the messy details."

"I still can't believe he died like that," said Roylin. "It seems—"

"He was just a crazy old man, Roylin. Don't worry about it. He was a nuisance to himself and to everyone else." Tuttle reached out to put a consoling hand on Roylin's arm, but Roylin jumped back as if the venomous jaws of a snake were about to clamp onto him.

"Don't *ever* touch me!" he gasped.

"Have it your own way, boy," Tuttle said, a sneer turning his lip and revealing a gap-toothed smile. "Pleasant dreams!" Roylin turned and fled from the room, running for the stairs with Tuttle's awful laugh trailing him like acrid smoke.

When Roylin came into the apartment, his mother glared at him, her arms folded. "Where you been? You were supposed to be here right after school to baby-sit your brothers, remember? Now, I'm gonna be late for work!" she shouted. In shock about Mr. Miller's death, Roylin had forgotten that this was the one night each week that he and Amberlynn had to baby-sit their three younger brothers, Antwon, Chad, and Lonnie. Some nights, Darcy Wills or Tarah Carson came over to help watch the kids. "You better have a good excuse, boy. I know you ain't workin' tonight, so where you been?"

"Just leave me alone!" Roylin shouted, heading for his bedroom.

His mother stood in the hallway, blocking his escape. "Don't you talk to me in that tone of voice, boy. What's the matter with you?"

"Mom, just get off my case," Roylin yelled, dodging around her and running down the hall.

"Every day you gettin' more like your father!" she yelled after him.

Roylin slammed the door of his room. His mother's words haunted him. *Maybe she's right,* he thought. Screaming and slamming doors were common when his father was around. Now he was doing the same thing. Through the thin walls of the apartment, he could hear the sound of his youngest brother crying. The loud door slam must have awakened him.

Lying on his old mattress, Roylin felt more alone than he had ever felt in his life. From the living room, he could hear the muffled voices of his mother and sister. *They must be talking about me,* he thought. He tried not to think of what they would say if they knew about Tuttle and Mr. Miller. After the talking stopped, he heard the dull thud of the front door closing. His mother had left for work. In the silence of his bedroom, Roylin remembered the package he had placed under his mattress the day before.

Roylin quickly reached down and grabbed the small box. Carefully, he opened it and gently lifted out the necklace. The gold glimmered in the dim light of his room. If Korie had not wanted this necklace so badly, Roylin would not have gone into Mr. Miller's room and caused his death. But Roylin could not be mad at Korie. She was so beautiful, so sweet. Just thinking of her began to cool the fever of his anxiety. But then he remembered carrying Mr. Miller's body down to the dreary basement. Poor Mr. Miller. He always treated Roylin right. Roylin never would have hurt Mr. Miller, not for anything. But he did, and now there was no way to take it back.

Roylin slammed the palm of his hand against his forehead. He felt as if he were trapped in a horrible dream. It did not seem possible that Mr. Miller was dead and Roylin had caused it. *But it's all real,* Roylin thought, struggling to push the image of Mr. Miller's wrapped body out of his mind.

Roylin closed his eyes and tried to bring Korie's beautiful face to life before him. He tried to imagine how she would look when she first laid eyes on the necklace, how she would scream with delight. Roylin finally fell asleep thinking of Korie, but he dreamed about Mr. Miller.

In his dream, he was a small boy again, nine or ten, and he was in Mr. Miller's apartment. The two of them were playing with the tiny cars. Roylin felt so safe and happy there. Mr. Miller was like an ever-patient doting grandfather one minute and like a little boy the next. He and Roylin pretended all the little cars were traveling across the floor in a great traffic jam, and he did not mind the mess they made. Roylin always looked forward to escaping from his yelling, cursing, hitting father to this oasis of peace and fun.

"I'm sorry, Mr. Miller," Roylin cried out in his dream. The cry woke him up. He was lying in the pitch black of his bedroom, and his face was wet with tears. Roylin had not cried in such a long time. The last time was when he was five years old and his finger almost got smashed in a slammed car door. After that, Roylin never cried again. Even when his father stood him against the door and whipped him, he did not cry. Even when he got shot, he did not cry. But now Roylin wept.

For the first time in his life he felt an overwhelming sense of guilt. He had done bad things before—he had stolen small items from the dollar store; he had taunted kids at Bluford, like girls who weighed too much and kids with skin problems. Not long ago, he had even teased Hakeem about his stuttering. In the past, Roylin could laugh off his behavior. But now everything was different.

Ambrose Miller was dead, and Roylin was to blame. And now, that good man would be buried under a concrete slab in a dank basement. There would not even be a funeral. Not even a little marker telling when Ambrose Miller died or a little cross carved in the stone. Just a piece of dank ground in that basement room with nobody to grieve or even to know.

Roylin got out of bed and went to the window. He felt sick. His head pounded and his stomach hurt. He wished *he* were dead instead of Mr. Miller.

In the morning, Roylin managed to eat some oatmeal. Then he fled as Mom was coaxing food into the boys and the baby. He could not stand being around his family now because he felt so evil. His little brothers' innocent faces reproached him. He felt like a monster in the midst of his family.

I'm worse than Dad, Roylin thought as he drove to school. *At least he never killed anybody.*

When Roylin walked into history class early for a change, Cooper greeted him cheerfully. "Hey Roylin, you turn over a new leaf or something? We got five whole minutes till Ms. Eckerly gets here."

"Don't mess with me right now, Cooper," Roylin said.

Cooper's eyes grew huge, like full moons in his dark face. "Man! You give a dude a compliment, and he like to chew your head off! What's wrong with you, Roylin? You drop outta bed on the wrong side or somethin'?"

"Maybe the cops are after him," Steve Morris said, laughing.

Roylin spun around, terror clawing at him, "Whatta you sayin' that for? You don't know nothin' about me! Why you talkin' trash about me? You want to get beat down?"

"Hey, you guys," Hakeem said, "just cool it, okay? Nobody wants trouble."

Roylin saw Darcy exchange a look of surprise with Hakeem. He could tell the other kids were looking at him as if he were crazy. He did not care. Right now, he felt like a ticking time bomb, ready to explode.

Chapter 5

Korie Archer came into the classroom, wearing a pair of jeans that rested perfectly on her curved hips. Her small T-shirt clung tightly to her body. She looked at Roylin and said, "Hey, is this seat taken?"

Roylin felt instant meltdown. Smiling back at Korie, he said, "It's all yours!" With her next to him, he was able to forget Mr. Miller, Tuttle, and his problems at home.

"Listen to the lovebirds," Tarah Carson snickered. "Boy, Korie, you sure got him trained!"

Korie giggled and said, "Oh, you just don't understand him. He's a pussycat." She reached over with her soft hand and rubbed Roylin's neck. "Aren't you, Roylin?"

Roylin shrugged his shoulders sheepishly and looked down at the ground. "Whatever you say, Korie," he said.

"I can't wait to see my surprise," she continued. "It's all I've been able to think about, and I'm starting to come up with ideas. If it's what I think it is, I'll just faint in your arms, I know it."

Roylin smiled. Here, sitting beside Korie in the sunny classroom, it seemed so much easier to dismiss all that had happened in the apartment. He never meant to hurt Mr. Miller. He had just borrowed some money. Mr. Miller would not have minded that. Roylin would have paid it back, except that before he could, Mr. Miller died of old age, that was all. How was that Roylin's fault? Maybe it was not even the missing money that triggered the heart attack. How could that old devil Tuttle know that for sure? If Mr. Miller was babbling about missing money, it might have been just a coincidence. Tuttle himself said Mr. Miller was demented. Maybe he did not even know what he was talking about.

The death of Mr. Miller seemed to dissolve as Korie's warm hand rested on Roylin's shoulder, then on his knee. Roylin began daydreaming about their

46

future together, the dates at the beach, how proud he would be taking her to school dances.

After Korie left for her next class and Roylin was walking alone in the hallway, Hakeem fell in stride beside him. "Man, it's none of my business, but that girl seems to come on awful strong, you know what I mean?"

Roylin turned and glared at Hakeem, "You jealous? You mad 'cause she's not comin' on to you?"

"You know Darcy and I got a good thing going. Look, Roylin, you and I have never been close friends, but as one guy to another, there's something about that girl I don't like."

"Shows you don't know anything, man," Roylin said. "Korie is the most honest girl I ever knew. She tells a guy just what she's thinkin', not playin' games with your mind like a lot of girls do. She don't make you crawl just to get a lousy date."

"Okay, Roylin," Hakeem said. Then he went ahead to join up with Darcy.

When Roylin got home from school, he found Tuttle waiting for him. "What do *you* want?" Roylin almost spat out the question.

"Get off your high horse, boy," Tuttle said calmly. "My arthritis is kickin' up, and the first and second floor hallways need moppin' and shinin' up. Folks spill drinks, stuff like that. Some tenants are givin' me trouble about the dirty hallways, so why don't you take care of that for me."

"What? Listen, Tuttle, I gotta work tonight! I gotta be there at 5:30!"

Tuttle looked at his watch, "Well, that means you best start crackin', boy. It's 4:00 and you need to shine up two long hallways real fast if you want time to grab some dinner."

"I can't do no work for you now, you—" Roylin began, his anger boiling over.

"Watch it, boy," Tuttle warned. "I'm going to have to work very hard buryin' our friend Ambrose. The cement has to be cracked, the dirt is hard, and I want to go deep enough. I just don't have time to do the halls too. Now, if you prefer, I could just call the police and tell them what happened, and . . ."

"Okay, okay. I'll do the halls!" Roylin snapped.

"That's better. By the way," Tuttle added, "I thought you might want this. Mr. Miller told me once how much you liked this one." He handed Roylin a match box.

Roylin took the box reluctantly from Tuttle's grimy hands. He slid the container open and gasped when he saw the tiny Porsche he had so often played with. Roylin threw it back at Tuttle, and it landed on the floor between them. Tuttle smirked, stooped and picked it up. "The guilt is eatin' you alive, isn't it, Roylin? I used to be like that. When I was very young, before life hardened me, the guilt would gnaw at me too. Don't worry about it. As time goes by, you'll care less. You'll be able to remember Ambrose Miller and laugh at what a useless old fool he was."

"Just shut up!" Roylin cried. "Don't say anything! Just get out of my sight, okay? I'll do the floors, and then you leave me alone, okay?"

Tuttle stood there for a moment smiling, seeming to enjoy Roylin's misery.

Roylin rushed through the job of cleaning and waxing the hallways. Amberlynn saw him when she came home from school and asked, "What're you doing, Roylin? Are you Tuttle's assistant now?"

"Girl, can't you just shut up for once!" Roylin yelled.

"Why are you being so mean?" Amberlynn challenged. "I hate you so much. You're just like Tuttle. I wish he would adopt you so you could go live down there with him in the basement!"

Roylin snapped. Mr. Miller's death, Amberlynn's harsh words, and her angry face were too much. Instantly, all his thoughts dissolved and were replaced with a blind, mind-numbing rage. In one quick motion, he grabbed the bucket of dirty, soapy water and poured it on his sister's head.

"Roylin!" Amberlynn screamed, her hair, shirt, and jeans soaked in the filthy brown water. "I HATE you!" she yelled, as she turned back into the apartment and slammed the door, leaving him alone in the hallway.

When Roylin cleaned the spilled water and put the mop away, he returned to the apartment. His mother confronted him as soon as he walked in.

"Roylin Bailey, what has gotten into you?" she yelled. "Don't you ever touch your sister! You hear me?! Don't you *ever!*"

"She likes to mock me, Mom. She all the time tauntin' me and dissin' me, and I can't take it no more. She wishin' me dead and stuff like that," Roylin lied. "So I lost it and threw water at her. I'm sorry, Mom, but she was askin' for it."

"Roylin, do something like that again, and you ain't livin' here," his mother said. "It'd break my heart to send you away, 'cause you are my child, but I'll do it if you don't learn to control yourself. You know I sent your daddy away, and I'll send you away too, you hear me?"

"I'm sorry, Mom," Roylin said.

"You better be. And the next time, 'sorry' won't fix it, you hear? I got me a bad feelin', Roylin. You going down the same road your daddy went. You gonna end up in a steel cage in state prison just like him, just like your daddy. I got this terrible feelin'."

Perspiration ran down Roylin's body as he retreated to his room. "Don't say that, Mom. Don't say that," he pleaded to himself.

As Roylin prepared to leave for work at the Golden Grill, Darcy Wills arrived to baby-sit the younger children. "Hi, Darcy," Mrs. Bailey said warmly as Antwon and Chad ran over and hugged Darcy's legs. "The baby's asleep, and everybody's already eaten dinner." As Mrs. Bailey walked out the door, she delivered the usual warnings to Antwon and Chad to behave.

"Hi, Darcy," Amberlynn said as she entered the room. Something seemed to catch her eye. "Ooh, let me see!" she exclaimed, pointing at the gold charm on Darcy's bracelet.

"It's an 'H,'" Darcy said. "Hakeem gave it to me."

"It's really pretty," Amberlynn said.

"I bet Hakeem got it at the dollar store," Roylin interrupted. "You shoulda dated me when I asked you, Darcy. Remember when I asked you out and you blew me off? I wouldn't be giving you some cheap trinket like that."

Annoyance darkened Darcy's face, but she said only, "Like they say, it's the thought that counts. Not the price."

"You wanna see what I'm getting for my girl?" Roylin asked.

Darcy shrugged, sitting on the floor to help Chad with his puzzle. "If you want to show me."

Roylin went to his room and brought out the box containing the necklace. He crouched on the floor beside Darcy and held up the necklace. The gold chain draped itself over his fingers, and the pendant with the tiny diamond chips and ruby glowed in the lamplight. Seeing the beautiful, shiny object, Chad forgot all about the jigsaw puzzle and grabbed for it.

"Get away!" Roylin exploded. "Keep your dirty fingers off. This is for someone special, and she's the only one who gets to hold it."

"Oh my goodness!" Amberlynn squealed. "Where did you get the money to buy something like that?"

"Don't worry about it," Roylin snapped.

He turned to Darcy and was pleased to see her eyes widen. She looked mesmerized by the diamonds and the ruby.

"Now aren't you sorry you're not my girl?" Roylin challenged Darcy.

Darcy smiled. "Roylin, you know I'm happy with Hakeem. No necklace is gonna change my mind about that." She looked closely at the pendant. "Still, that's a really pretty gift."

"You got no idea what it cost me," Roylin went on, after putting the necklace back in its box and returning it to his room.

"A lot, I guess," Darcy said as she pushed a puzzle piece towards Chad.

"Three hundred dollars," Roylin bragged. "Yeah! Three hundred dollars. But Korie Archer, she's worth it. I'm tellin' you, she's so crazy about me she can't keep her hands off me!"

"Well I'm glad you two are happy," Darcy said. "Really, I—"

"Happy ain't the word. It's better than that, but I guess you'll never know." With those words, Roylin left, puffed with pride.

Chapter 6

The following afternoon, Tuttle was waiting for Roylin again when he came home from school.

"Man, I wish you'd leave me alone!" Roylin snarled.

"Somebody's gotta clean out the old man's room so I can rent it to somebody else. The landlord is screamin' for a new tenant. You don't make money on an empty apartment," Tuttle said. "I just about finished breakin' the cement, and I scratched the soil a bit, but I'm a long way from making a hole big enough to bury a body. I need you to clear the room."

"I c-can't go in there," Roylin stammered.

Tuttle straightened his dirty baseball cap. "Just clean up the mess. I got rid of the little cars, but he left a lot of junk, papers, clippings and letters. Just bundle it all in trash bags, and then tidy things up. Shouldn't take you more than an hour."

"I told you," Roylin repeated, "I can't go in there."

"Well then, would you like to come down to the basement and dig the grave, boy?" Tuttle asked, a mocking smile on his face. "It's either that or tidy up the room."

"Okay," Roylin whispered, fighting waves of nausea that swept over him.

Roylin went into the apartment he had entered so many times before. Filled with the aroma of vanilla air freshener, the room still smelled as if Mr. Miller had never left. Even though he was old and frail, Mr. Miller always kept his apartment clean. Roylin shuddered as he stepped into the living room. His throat tightened, and he decided to quickly toss everything in a garbage bag and get out fast.

The carpet where Roylin and Mr. Miller played with the little cars was now faded and worn. Roylin stared at the geometric patterns and remembered driving the toy cars along the rug's shapes and lines many years ago. Over in the corner were piles of newspapers. Mr. Miller loved to read. Roylin got rid of the newspapers quickly, and then he tackled the closet. Mr. Miller's clothing was gone. He did not have much, just a few shirts, a few pairs of pants. Tuttle probably put the clothes in a dumpster.

Roylin remembered it then—the cardigan sweater he had bought for Mr. Miller the Christmas Roylin was eleven. Roylin saved money from his odd jobs and went to a thrift store and got Mr. Miller a nice cardigan sweater with a red and white pattern on it. How touched Mr. Miller had been by the gift. How proud Roylin had felt to give it to him, even though it was only a used sweater from the thrift store. It was the one gift Roylin gave that meant more to his old friend than anything else. Roylin felt his chest tighten.

At the bottom of the closet were old shoe boxes where Mr. Miller kept odds and ends. He called the boxes his "treasure chests." He would often take out a "treasure," such as a yo-yo or stopwatch, for them to enjoy. And around Christmas, he would always give Roylin something from his boxes. Sometimes that was the only gift Roylin got.

Roylin was tempted to toss the boxes into plastic garbage bags. But something stopped him. His hands trembled as he opened one of the boxes and found a bundle of greeting cards tied with rubber bands. When he took off the bands, the cards fell into his lap. All bore childish handwriting.

"To my friend, Mr. Miller, your friend, Roylin," most of the cards read. Some even had pictures drawn on them. Looking at them, Roylin felt as if someone had driven a stake through his heart. Mr. Miller had saved all those stupid cards Roylin had given him. He saved them like they were important. They meant that much to him.

The room turned black around Roylin, and he thought he would pass out. Suddenly he was mumbling to himself, "I'm sorry, Mr. Miller. I didn't mean to make you die, I didn't mean to . . ." Roylin remembered hearing once that good people go to heaven after they die, and then they can hear what people say on earth. Mr. Miller was a good man. He never hurt anybody. He delivered mail for forty years, and he was married almost that long, until his wife died. He had a daughter, but she moved across the country and mostly ignored him. Mr. Miller was the closest thing Roylin ever had to a loving father. He was the one man who kept Roylin from being totally alone during the violent and frightening years of his childhood. So Roylin hoped that Mr. Miller was somewhere good now and that he could hear Roylin's anguished voice. "I'm sorry, Mr. Miller, I'm sorry. Please hear me. Please forgive me. I didn't mean to make you die."

Roylin grabbed the bundle of cards and stuffed it in a garbage bag, but then he stopped and drew it out again. Destroying everything Mr. Miller left would be like killing him all over again. Roylin shook as he put the cards in a separate bag, one he would not put out in the trash. Roylin put the contents of Mr. Miller's other treasure boxes in that separate bag too. He saved all the little things that Mr. Miller valued, the cheap cuff links, the baseball cards, the stupid little gifts Roylin had given him over the years. Then Roylin vacuumed the worn rug and did a quick wipe up in the kitchen and bathroom.

He rushed out and disposed of the trash, but he took the mementos upstairs to his room. He stuffed the bag in the back of his closet. As he did that, he heard a strange sound from the basement, like a metal shovel hitting the dirt.

"Been listening to that most of the day," he heard his mother complain. "Tuttle is diggin' down there. What on earth could that man be doing?"

"Maybe he's fixing our pipes so we have hot water," Amberlynn said.

Roylin cringed. Tuttle was digging Mr. Miller's grave. That is what he was doing. Suddenly, Roylin felt he had to get out of the apartment. He did not have to work tonight, but he had to get away from that haunting sound. He stuffed the box containing the necklace in his jacket pocket.

"Gotta see a man about a job," Roylin said before he took off. If he was lucky, he could get together with Korie. He had to be with her tonight. Seeing her would be the only thing that could make him feel better. He could not wait anymore for some romantic dinner in a restaurant. He needed to see her.

Roylin stopped at a pay phone and dialed her number. He was relieved when she answered. "Korie," he said, "it's Roylin. Listen, I gotta see you tonight. I just gotta."

"You mean right now?" Korie asked.

"I'm feelin' really low and I need you right now, okay?" Roylin said desperately.

"Oh man, Roylin, I'm swamped with homework, and I got that horrible history paper about a stupid Civil War general. Mom expects me to stay home and do schoolwork. She's not home right now, but when she gets in, she'll check on me like a jail warden!"

"Please, Korie. I got something for you. You won't be sorry," Roylin begged.

"Well . . . okay," she replied. "If you pick me up, and we just spend a little time together, I guess it's okay."

"I'll be right over," Roylin said. He hung up the phone and ran to the Honda. His mind filled with fantasies of how Korie would react when she saw the necklace. In all his excitement, Roylin almost forgot about the thud of Tuttle's shovel digging into the ground somewhere in the distance.

Korie came running when Roylin honked his horn. She was wearing faded jeans and a beat-up black sweatshirt. But even though the clothes were old, she looked fantastic. "Hi, Roylin," she

61

said, getting in. "How come you're feeling so low? What's the matter?"

"Nothing the matter now that you're with me," Roylin said. "I'll drive over to Niko's pizza place, and we can park there."

"I'm not hungry, Roylin. I already ate dinner and I'm stuffed," Korie said. "You said you had something for me?"

"We'll just park, and yeah, I have something for you!" Roylin swerved into the far end of a nearby parking lot. He flipped on the light inside the car and fumbled inside his jacket for the box. Slowly he brought it out.

"What's *that?*" Korie asked, her eyes growing huge.

"What do you think it is?" Roylin asked.

"I . . . I don't know. Oh Roylin, you didn't, did you? Oh my goodness! Let me see, let me see!" Korie trembled with anticipation.

Roylin held the gift box in the air, beyond her reach. Korie grabbed for it, laughing. Finally her hand closed around it. She yanked off the lid, letting it fall to the floor of the car. Quickly her hands were inside the box, eagerly pulling away the delicate cotton padding that covered its contents. When she saw the necklace, she screamed. The howl of delight filled the inside of the car.

"Oh Roylin! Oh, thank you, thank you! I never dreamed I'd ever really have this. Oh, thank you!" Korie threw her arms around Roylin's neck and kissed him all over his face. Then she returned her attention to the necklace, putting it on and twisting to see herself in the rear-view mirror. "Ohhhh, I feel like a princess!"

Roylin grinned happily. "You like it? It's the best gift you ever got, huh?"

"Oh Roylin, I never in my whole life got such a gift! Oh, I love you so much. You are the greatest guy in the whole world!" Korie raved, hugging the necklace to herself. She kissed Roylin again, and for several minutes, Roylin felt more happiness than he had ever imagined. But then Korie looked at her watch and said, "Oh no! Mom will be home any minute! If she finds me gone, she'll kill me!"

"It's okay. I'll drive you home right away," Roylin said.

"We can be together this weekend. Oh Roylin, I love you!" Korie cried.

"Love you too, Korie." Roylin leaned over and kissed her as he drove.

Once more, before she left the car, Korie kissed Roylin, but when he clung to her, she pulled away. "Mom is gonna be home, and if she catches me not doing my homework, I'm dead! Roylin, I'm already falling behind in two subjects, and Mom says if I don't shape up, I'm grounded forever!"

Korie ran for her front door, stopping once to blow Roylin a goodnight kiss before she disappeared inside.

And then Roylin was alone again in his car. She was gone. He was swept by a terrible emptiness. Everything he had lived for during the past few days had disappeared. The excitement of buying Korie the necklace, the thrill of giving it to her, the fantasies about what she would do and say—they were all over now. Korie had her necklace. She had thanked Roylin, but still he was alone in the early evening darkness.

Chapter 7

At the corner of the street near Korie's apartment, Roylin saw some boys from Bluford. None of them were his friends, but he knew who they were. Bobby Wallace was there, leaning on his car with Shanetta Greene and some other troublemakers from Bluford. Some of the kids stared at Roylin as he drove by. A fresh wave of depression swept over him. He did not fit in with thugs like Bobby and Londell James. He was scared stiff of them. He did not fit in with the nice, smart kids like Hakeem. He did not fit in with jocks like Cooper Hodden who did great things on the football field. Roylin never felt he fit in with anybody. He was a below-average student, a mediocre athlete, a social outcast. He was the kid from the family with the crazy dad who yelled and broke things so often that Roylin never dared to have a friend over.

When Roylin got home, his phone was ringing. Darcy answered it. She had put the younger children to bed, and Amberlynn was staying over at Darcy's house with her younger sister, Jamee.

"It's for you, Roylin," Darcy said, returning to the kitchen to clean up the last of the dinner mess before she went home.

"Hi, Roylin," Korie said in a frantic voice. "Oh, you gotta help me. Our history paper is due in three days, and I haven't even started it. Mom says if I get lower than a B in any of my classes, she'll ground me."

Roylin was disappointed that she did not say anything about the necklace. He had given it to her a little more than an hour ago, and already she was on to something else. "You still like your necklace, don't you?" he asked.

"Sure I do, Roylin! I adore it! And I'll love you forever and ever for getting it for me, but if I don't do well on this history paper, we won't be able to go out together. Mom will ground me for a hundred years!"

"Man, Korie, I'm lousy in history too. I got a D minus in that class. I already did my paper for Eckerly, but I'll be lucky if I get a C," Roylin said.

"Do you know *anybody* who'd do my paper for me, Roylin?" Korie pleaded. Just then Roylin heard Darcy rattling around the pots and pans in the kitchen.

"I'll call you back, Korie. I got an idea," Roylin said. After he hung up, he went into the kitchen. "Hey, Darcy, you wanna do me the biggest favor in the world?" he asked.

Darcy smiled and put the casserole dish away. "If I can, sure," she said.

"You know Korie Archer?"

"Yeah."

"She's my girl now, and Eckerly assigned that huge history paper, and she just can't do it. You get good grades, Darcy. You could knock out a paper for Korie without any sweat," Roylin said.

"I'd be glad to work with Korie tomorrow at lunch and after school too. I'll show her how I did mine and—"

"No," Roylin cut in, "she needs somebody to *do* the paper 'cause she's lousy at this kind of stuff, and this huge history paper is just impossible. All you'd have to do is just write it up on the computer at school and put her name on it."

"Roylin, it's not a huge paper. It's just three pages. And I won't write it for her and put her name on it. We'd both get in trouble."

"Please, Darcy. You gotta do it for me. I got all kinds of problems, and if something goes wrong with me and Korie, I couldn't take it, okay?"

"Roylin, tomorrow at lunch I'll work with Korie—" Darcy said.

"Me and Korie have lunch together. That's our time. I can't have her working with you. That's *our time*, don't you see?"

Darcy rolled her eyes. "Roylin, are you crazy?! What's wrong with you? You can spare one lunch hour with Korie!"

"No, see, Korie can't do it. Listen, if I gave you the name of the general in the Civil War that she has to do the paper on, if you could just write the paper up, Darcy, I'd pay you. Yeah, I would. How much do you want?" Roylin said.

"Roylin, there is no way I'm gonna do something like that. It's cheating and I'm not gonna do it, okay?" Darcy yelled, losing her temper.

"You're such a goody-goody that you won't do me this one little favor?" Roylin pleaded.

"I'm not writing a paper and letting Korie put her name on it. Ms. Eckerly will bust us both! It's just not happening," Darcy said.

"Girl, I can't believe you," Roylin yelled, realizing Darcy would not change her mind. "Don't you *ever* ask me for a favor!"

Roylin returned to the hall and called Korie. Korie spoke excitedly when she heard his voice. "Roylin, did you find somebody to do my paper?"

"Listen. There's this girl who can help you write the paper. She'll sit with you and go over it step by step. She's really smart, and I know you'd be okay doin' it if she helped you," Roylin said.

"Roylin! I just can't do it. I hate history! I can't write a decent sentence. I don't care how much help I get! Don't you understand? If I write the report I'll flunk history. Roylin, I'm desperate!" Korie cried.

"Relax, baby. I'll ask around tomorrow. I'm sure I can get somebody to do your report for you," Roylin promised.

"Okay. Oh! Mom's coming in. Bye!"

Roylin put the phone down slowly. Korie did not even say 'love ya' or anything. It was as if Roylin had never even bought her the necklace for three hundred dollars. It was as if the thing he did—stealing from poor old Ambrose Miller and causing his death—had been for nothing. Roylin would never completely forget what happened to Mr. Miller. It would remain a dark, painful shadow over the rest of his life, no matter how hard he tried to push it away. But he had convinced himself that his gift to Korie would cement their relationship so firmly that he would have this incredible girl in his life forever. And, somehow, that would even things up. But now he had the awful feeling that he was wrong. What if the gift was not enough? Maybe Korie desired the necklace in the same way a child wants a shiny ornament on a Christmas tree. And now that she had it, he thought, she might turn her attention to something else. But what?

Roylin's mother came home and made small talk with Darcy for a few minutes. Then Darcy left, and Mom pulled off her heavy overcoat. "It's so cold where I work. I'm just cold to the bone. Well, Roylin, you have a good day?"

"Yeah, sure," Roylin lied. "I'm tired, though. I'm gonna go to bed." Roylin hurried to his room and closed the door. He fell into a fitful sleep and kept waking up all night, sometimes in a cold sweat. He thought he heard Tuttle chopping at the hard ground in the basement, trying to make a hole big enough to bury Mr. Miller.

At school the next morning, Roylin looked for Korie. He found her talking to Steve Morris.

"What do *you* want?" Roylin growled, looking at Steve.

"Roylin!" Korie exclaimed, "Steve is gonna do my paper for me. Isn't that great?"

Roylin's heart sank. Now Steve would have a claim on Korie too. "You ain't smart enough to do Korie's history report," Roylin said. "All you know how to do is play football. You're just a jock, and all jocks are stupid."

"Look who's talking!" Steve sneered. "You're lucky you didn't get kicked off the team with the grades you got. I'm gettin' a B plus in history. I know that's better than you."

Before Roylin could respond, Korie cut in, putting her hand on his arm. "Hey, Roylin, don't be mad. Steve is just doing me a favor. You do want me to pass history, don't you?"

"You think you *own* Korie?" Steve laughed, his eyes narrowing. "Nobody owns anybody else. You better deal with that."

Roylin glared at Steve Morris with hatred, but he did not know what to do about it. He turned and walked towards the history classroom. In a moment Korie caught up to him.

"Please don't be mad, Roylin," Korie said.

"Mad? Girl, do you know what I went through to get that necklace? Ever since you got it, you ain't done nothin' except treat me like garbage. Give me one reason why I shouldn't be mad?" Roylin said bitterly.

"Roylin! I told you I loved the necklace. Anyway, you said you had plenty of money, that you're always buying expensive gifts. Was that a lie?"

"No, it's just that I really went out of my way to get you what you wanted, and now it's like it never happened," Roylin said resentfully. "You're hanging on Steve Morris and treating me like yesterday's newspaper."

"I am not treating you that way, Roylin. I don't understand what's wrong with you. You *know* I need somebody to

72

do my paper, and Steve said he would. I think that's very nice. What's your problem?" Korie demanded.

Roylin turned and stormed off, deciding to skip history. He got an excuse slip by telling the school nurse he felt sick. He could not sit in that classroom today with Korie smiling at Steve.

After history class, Roylin ran into Cooper in the hallway.

"Man, girls ain't nothin' but trouble," Roylin fumed to Cooper.

Cooper laughed. "You just findin' that out? You didn't figure that out in first grade?"

"I gave Korie Archer this beautiful necklace for her birthday, and now she's flirtin' with Steve Morris," Roylin complained. It was not like him to discuss his personal problems with anybody. When he was hurting, he always tried to hurt somebody else. But Roylin hurt now more than he ever did in his life.

"Say what?" Cooper gasped. "You gave that new girl a necklace already?"

"Yeah, and now she's dumping me for Morris!"

"Man, Morris is smooth. He's always got girls chasin' him. If you think you can win her from Morris with some cheap jewelry, you got another thing comin'," Cooper said.

"Coop, it wasn't cheap. I paid three hundred dollars for that necklace," Roylin said.

"What?!" Cooper gasped in astonishment. "How much?"

"Three hundred bucks. That's a month of tips at the Golden Grill just so she can have that necklace on her neck," Roylin sighed.

"Man, you the craziest dude I ever met," Cooper replied. "Tarah Carson is my girl, and she'd do anything for me, and I'd do anything for her. But the most I ever paid for a gift for her was twenty bucks!"

"We ain't talkin' about just any girl, Coop. This is Korie Archer. Have you taken a good *look* at her? She is the best. She's the sports car guys dream about, but never get to touch."

Cooper shook his head. "Know what, man? I wouldn't take six Korie Archers for one Tarah Carson, you know what I'm sayin'? Tarah is there for me, and she always gonna be. And she got heart. "

Roylin shrugged. Tarah Carson was a big girl. She had a pretty face, but she could not compare to Korie. "Coop, I'm tellin' you, my life is a mess!" Roylin said with deep sadness.

"Hey, man, you ain't usin', are you?" Cooper asked suddenly.

"Drugs? No way. Are you crazy?" Roylin exclaimed.

"Well, whatever's goin' on, just know I got your back. We're friends, yo. You hear me?"

Roylin could not believe what Cooper had just said. In his entire life, nobody except Mr. Miller had ever considered Roylin a friend. Roylin was deeply touched by Cooper's simple words. But if Cooper knew what he had done, he never would have called him a friend.

Chapter 8

"Thanks for listenin', man," Roylin said, shaking Cooper's hand.

"Listen up, Roylin," Cooper said. "You been actin' like somebody is following you or something. Just a feelin' I got. Anytime anything on your mind, you can tell me about it, okay? It won't go no further, you hear me? I'll help any way I can. I kinda know where you're comin' from. My house ain't exactly paradise either."

Roylin nodded. He remembered from middle school how Cooper sometimes came to school with bruises. At the time, everyone at school talked about Cooper's abusive stepfather. Roylin figured that kids talked about his dad in the same way.

But that was years ago. And Cooper seemed clever enough to avoid much of that now. He was so good-natured that he could take a bad situation and make it bearable. Once Roylin heard Tarah say of Cooper, *"That boy can take the sourest mess of lemons and come up with the sweetest lemonade."*

But Roylin was not like Cooper. Roylin's nature ran to bitter, like his father's. It seemed to Roylin that the cards were stacked against him, that there was something about him that was unlovable. As a small boy, Roylin figured that was why his father beat him all the time—because he, Roylin Bailey, was worthless. All morning, Roylin thought about Cooper's words, marveling about them over and over again.

"Anytime anything on your mind, you can tell me about it, okay?" Amazingly, Cooper was offering friendship. Roylin shook his head. *The only friend I ever had was Mr. Miller, and look what happened to him,* Roylin thought sadly. *Cooper better stay away from me.*

At lunchtime, Roylin went to meet Korie. She came out of the classroom with Steve. "Oh Roylin," she called, seeing him, "I can't go to lunch with you today. I'm showing Steve what I have to do on that paper so he can get started."

Steve winked at Roylin behind Korie's back. His wink said, *"You're out of the picture, man. You're history, Roylin. Sit back and watch as I walk away with your girl."*

Roylin did not say a word. He didn't have the heart to go into the cafeteria for a hot meal, so he bought a stale sandwich from one of the snack machines. Then he went outside, hoping some fresh air would calm him down. But he looked down at the sandwich, then smashed it against the bark of a tree. Blood streamed over his knuckles, but he felt no pain from his bruised hand. The pain inside him was so great that he could not feel anything else.

On Saturday afternoon, as Roylin was leaving to meet Korie, Tuttle confronted him.

"Got a lot of paintin' to do, boy," Tuttle said. "Gotta be done this weekend so that the front of this dump looks good. Owner is comin' by to look things over."

"I don't paint," Roylin snarled.

Tuttle cackled and then said softly, "I finished the hole. Want to see it before I put him in?"

Roylin groaned in horror. An image of Mr. Miller's crumpled body lying on the floor of Tuttle's basement flashed in his mind. He felt a sickening feeling in his stomach, and his body trembled. Tuttle crept closer.

"Are you forgettin' our arrangement, boy?" Tuttle sneered. "I got the evidence to put you behind bars for the rest of your natural life. Remember?"

The words were too much for Roylin. He cowered away from Tuttle and raised his hands to his ears in an attempt to block the sound of Tuttle's voice—just as he did years earlier to escape the noise of his father screaming at his mother.

"Now, you gonna do some paintin', and it's gonna be done before tomorrow night, you got that?" Tuttle growled, making sure Roylin would hear him even with his hands over his ears.

Waves of fear and hatred washed over Roylin. "I can't do it now. I'll do it later on today," he whispered.

"That's fine with me, but if it don't get done . . . " Tuttle pressed his own hands together as if they were hand-cuffed. "Click-click." Then he chuckled again, turned his old Dodgers cap around, and walked off.

Roylin went to his Honda and took off. Korie had promised he could pick her up and they would do something together. Maybe they would go to the beach and then grab some burgers. Roylin was really looking forward to it. Thinking about it was all that kept him from going crazy.

Roylin pulled up in front of the apartment where Korie lived and hit the horn. That is what Korie told him to do. Korie did not want to introduce him to her parents, she said, because they did not want her to date until she was seventeen.

Korie did not appear, so Roylin hit the horn again. Still she did not come. Roylin got out of the car and went to her apartment, finally ringing the bell at 3B. A very attractive woman answered. She said she was Korie's mother and Korie was not at home. "She went to a girlfriend's house to work on a school project," the woman said, her eyes narrowing. "Who are you anyway?"

"Just a guy from her class. I was gonna work on the project too. Do you know what house she's at?" Roylin asked.

Korie's mother checked a pad near the phone. "She said she was going to study with Brisana Meeks. Do you know where she lives?"

"Yeah, I do. Thanks," Roylin said, hurrying away. Roylin had never been to Brisana's house. It was in a much better neighborhood at the edge of the area served by Bluford High. Most Bluford students lived in old houses or in apartment projects built by the government, but a new housing development had been built featuring nice condos. Brisana lived in one of the newest units, and her house had a small front yard with a few flowering bushes. As Roylin pulled up to the house, his mind was spinning again. Maybe Korie wanted him to meet her here so her mother would not see him. But then why didn't she tell him that?

Brisana came to the door. She looked Roylin up and down with clear distaste, as someone might look at a nasty bug on the wall. "What are *you* doing here?" she asked coldly.

"I think my girlfriend is over here studyin'," Roylin stammered. "You know, Korie Archer."

"*Your* girlfriend?" Brisana said, smiling at Roylin as if he were a three-year old kid who still believed in Santa Claus.

"Would you just tell her I'm here, so we can go?"

"She's not here," Brisana replied.

"Yeah, she is," Roylin argued. "Her mother said she was studyin' with you." Roylin tried to look past Brisana into the condo. "Korie! I'm here!"

"Roylin, you are pathetic," Brisana said. "Don't you understand that Korie told her mom she was studying here so she and Steve could go out? I mean Korie's mom has no clue what Korie does. All she cares about is keeping Korie in the house. Anyway, Steve came and picked her up an hour ago."

Roylin turned cold. He felt as if he was standing in ice water up to his neck. "Why are you lyin' to me?" he gasped. "Korie said we were goin' out this afternoon."

Brisana tossed her head impatiently. "Don't be stupid, Roylin. Just go home."

"Korie is my girl. She promised me we were going out together. She said she loved me, she said I was the greatest guy in the whole world . . . ," Roylin babbled. He knew he was making a complete fool of himself, but he could not help it.

"Roylin, just leave, okay? There isn't anything between you and Korie. There never was. Korie's with Steve. I don't know why you even thought you had a chance with her anyway," Brisana said.

Roylin turned and ran back to his car. He did not completely believe Brisana's story. How could Korie be doing something so cruel to him? The only way he would know the truth would be to find Korie and Steve together. He decided to drive through the neighborhood searching for Steve's black Cavalier. Roylin sped away from Brisana's and cruised past the hamburger and pizza joints for an hour, but he saw nothing. It was getting late, and he had to go home and do Tuttle's painting for him. Roylin was doing almost all of the old devil's work now and getting nothing for it. Desperation and hatred grew in Roylin's soul like wildfire. He wished Tuttle were dead. He wished he were dead himself.

Roylin was painting the front of the apartment building when Amberlynn came by. "How come you're doing all Tuttle's work now?" she asked.

"I'm pickin' up extra money," Roylin lied.

"Seems like you're working all the time. You must be getting rich," Amberlynn said.

"Get lost!" Roylin snapped.

But Amberlynn lingered. "What's the

matter with you, Roylin? You always had your bad moods, but sometimes you weren't so bad. Now you're mean all the time. You in trouble or something?"

"Girl, I told you to get lost," Roylin said.

"Roylin, everybody in the apartment is talking about how weird it was that Mr. Miller moved out so fast without even saying goodbye. Did he say goodbye to you? You were his friend, weren't you?"

"Don't you ever shut up?" Roylin snarled, slapping the paint on the boards and splashing himself.

"But you were Mr. Miller's friend. How come you didn't say he was moving?"

"I wasn't his friend." Perspiration began to run down Roylin's body. "I mean, not for a long time."

"You watched the Super Bowl with him last year," Amberlynn recalled.

"I did not. You're dreamin'!" Roylin insisted.

"You did. You even bought a big tin of popcorn just for the two of you. You seemed to like him a lot. Did you get his new address?" Amberlynn asked.

"Girl, mind your own business! Don't you have something better to do than bug me? Can't you see I'm busy?" Roylin cried.

Amberlynn refused to go away. "Seems like you should write him a note or something. You're acting like he's dead. Know what Mrs. Adams at the end of the hall said? She said he didn't move out at all. Maybe old Tuttle killed him. Ever since Mr. Miller went away, we've heard this weird sound from the basement like Tuttle is digging a grave or something. That's what Mrs. Adams says."

Terror struck Roylin. If talk like that spread, the police would come. There would be an investigation. It would take Tuttle about two seconds to turn Roylin in. Tuttle would be in trouble too for covering up what happened, but he would find a way to side with the law and be a witness against Roylin. Guys like Tuttle always landed on their feet. Roylin would be heading for state prison for murder. Being sixteen did not count for much anymore. In murder cases now, you were tried as an adult, and you ended up in adult prison.

"Listen, Mr. Miller went back East to stay with his daughter, okay? She came and picked him up, okay? That's all there is to it, so you can just tell that nosy old lady to forget about it," Roylin said.

85

"It just seems so sad to pass by his apartment and know he's not there anymore. I mean, he's had that place all my life. Mama said that if she'd known he was going, she woulda said goodbye too. She said that once when Daddy was hurting her real bad, she ran to Mr. Miller's apartment and he took her in. Did you know that, Roylin? Mama said he was such a fine man." Finally, then, Amberlynn walked away.

Roylin finished painting, cleaned up, and headed for his job at the Golden Grill. He was exhausted, but he had to go to work. If he did not show up for work on a busy Saturday night, he would get fired. All evening, customers poured in, and Roylin was glad of it. It helped him forget Mr. Miller's death and what Korie had done to him.

Finally, at midnight, Roylin took off his uniform and headed for the Honda. All he wanted to do was flop into bed and sleep. But, as he drove through the darkness towards home, he spotted Steve Morris's Cavalier parked near a small Chinese restaurant in the neighborhood. Roylin's blood began to boil. Was it possible that Korie and Steve had been together all day and now were having a romantic dinner? At this hour?

Roylin pulled into the parking lot some distance from the Cavalier. All the weariness he had felt earlier vanished as rage pumped him full of adrenalin. He waited, his eyes on the restaurant's red door. Finally it opened, and Korie and Steve came out together, their arms loosely linked. Korie was laughing, and they came together for a brief kiss. Then they strolled towards the car.

When the pair reached the Cavalier, Roylin got out of his car and walked towards Korie and Steve.

"Hi, Korie. I see you're wearin' that pretty necklace I gave you. It looks real nice, Korie."

"Roylin," Korie stammered, fear on her face, "what are you doing here?"

"Remember we had a date this afternoon? We were going to the beach and then out to eat, remember?" Roylin said bitterly.

"Oh!" Korie tried desperately to look surprised. "I completely forgot. See, Steve and I were working so hard at the library all day on that history paper, and just now we stopped to get something to eat. I'm so sorry, Roylin!"

"Liar," Roylin snarled, "rotten little liar!"

"Watch your mouth, man," Steve said sharply.

"I paid three hundred dollars for that necklace for your birthday, and you said you were gonna be my girl, and now you stabbed me in the back," Roylin screamed.

"Roylin, go home," Steve said. "You're drunk, or crazy."

Roylin glared with wild hatred at the big, handsome running back of the Bluford Buccaneers. Steve was the kind of guy who always won everything. Roylin always lost out to guys like him. Steve was smarter and better looking. Nothing ever went wrong in his life, Roylin figured. But for a little while, Roylin had been a winner. Sure, it cost him the life of the only friend he ever had. It cost him his peace of mind. And it put him in the clutches of Tuttle. But for a little while, Roylin was dating the most beautiful girl at Bluford High. He had stopped looking with envy at others—at guys like Steve. For once, they were casting envious eyes at him. But now that too was gone. The fantasy was over. The natural law was back in place. The Steve Morrises of the world were on top again, and Roylin was back where he belonged—at the bottom.

Roylin's fists tightened, and he lunged at Steve.

"I'll kill you!" he yelled.

"Roylin, *no!*" Korie cried.

Chapter 9

Steve Morris jumped aside, but Roylin caught his chin with his fist, sending him onto the ground with a heavy thud.

"Stop it!" Korie screamed.

Steve rolled over the minute he hit the dirt and scrambled to his feet. The boys scuffled in the darkness until Steve, heavier and stronger, wrenched Roylin's arm behind his back and yanked hard. Roylin screamed in pain. Steve released him and gave him a hard shove, sending Roylin tumbling forward until he crashed into a garbage can, then sank to the ground. The pain in Roylin's shoulder was so intense he almost passed out. Steve stood over him, glowering down. "Leave us alone, you understand? The next time you get in my face, I'll wrap you around a telephone pole!"

Steve grabbed Korie's hand, and they ran to the car together. In seconds, the Cavalier roared past Roylin as he lay in the debris by the garbage can.

Slowly the pain in Roylin's shoulder subsided. He got up, brushed the dirt off his clothing and staggered towards his car. Steve had beaten him, humiliated him in front of Korie. Not that it mattered anymore. Korie was gone. She had always been gone. Having her as a girlfriend was a cruel fantasy. Hakeem had been right when he took Roylin aside and warned him about Korie. Roylin saw it all clearly now. She wanted the necklace, and when Roylin started bragging about how rich he was, how he had money to burn, Korie went for it. She never really liked Roylin. She used him. Now that she had what she wanted, she went for the guy she really liked—Steve.

Roylin sat in his car, choked with sobs. He could not go on. He could not go home and wait for Tuttle to yank his chain every time he needed work done. He could not go back to school and watch Korie draped over Steve's arm. He could not take it anymore. He had nobody to turn to. Before, when things got rough at school or at home, there had always been Mr. Miller. He always understood. He always offered a shoulder to cry on, and he never betrayed Roylin. Now there was nobody to talk to.

Roylin thought he had no real friends at school. Guys like Hakeem tolerated him politely, probably pitied him. Deep down they did not like him. Who could blame them?

Darcy was the same way. To his face she acted friendly and polite, but Roylin could see in her eyes that she thought he was a loser. Why wouldn't she think that, he wondered. Every time he talked to her, he was rude or mean. He never let Darcy or anyone know how he really felt—scared, angry, and hurt. Instead, Roylin hid his feelings by acting tough, and now he had been doing it so long, he did not know how to do anything else. Roylin had never in his life felt so totally hopeless. He wished he could drop down a manhole and vanish into the city sewer where he felt he belonged.

And then, slowly, a face came to him, out of the darkness of his misery. The broad, warm face of Cooper Hodden. Cooper grinning and saying, *"Anytime anything on your mind, you can tell me about it."*

Cooper had said that, but had he meant it? Were those just empty words he threw at Roylin the way you'd throw a dog a bone? Were they empty words like those Korie used when she told Roylin she loved and adored him? If Roylin actually got in touch with Cooper, would Cooper think, "Oh man, don't tell me a loser is gonna latch onto me now! Why'd I tell him I gave a rat's behind about him? How am I gonna get rid of him now?" Roylin thought that was probably so, but he was not sure. Cooper Hodden was his last hope.

Roylin went to a nearby public phone and dialed Cooper's number.

The phone rang several times, and Roylin almost hung up. It was past midnight. Then a sleepy voice said, "Hello. You gotta have the wrong number 'cause nobody I know is stupid enough to call me this late."

"Cooper, it's Roylin. I gotta talk to somebody. Please," Roylin said.

"Say what?"

"Cooper, you said if I ever needed somebody to talk to . . . it's okay if you changed your mind, but I'm goin' down for the count, okay?" Roylin said, his voice shaking.

There was a brief silence at Cooper's end of the line. The sleepiness was gone from his voice when he said, "Where you at?"

"In the parking lot of the Jade Palace Chinese restaurant."

"I know where it's at. Hang on. I'll see you in fifteen minutes," Cooper said.

Roylin leaned against the Honda and waited. There was still a dull ache in his shoulder where Steve had twisted his arm. Roylin was not sure that Cooper would actually come, and when twenty minutes passed, Roylin figured Cooper had gone back to sleep. But then the familiar old pickup truck rattled into the parking lot, and Cooper jumped out.

"Hey, Roylin, what's goin' on? You sounded real serious on the phone." Cooper's big brown eyes were wide with concern. "Big Londell put a hit on you, or what?"

"My life's fallin' apart, and I don't know if I can go on," Roylin said softly.

"What are you talkin' 'bout, man?"

They sat down on the waist-high concrete wall that bordered the restaurant's parking lot, and Roylin said, "I just discovered Korie and Steve out together, holdin' hands, . . . kissin'. She was interested in the necklace I gave her, not in me."

"Oh, I'm sorry, man," Cooper said. "But there are other girls out there, you know."

"But that's not all, Coop. There's something worse. Much worse." Roylin stared down at the blacktop of the parking lot as he talked because he did not want to see the shock that would surely appear on Cooper's face. "Coop, there was this nice old man, Mr. Miller, living in the apartment building where I live, and we been friends since forever, you know? Anyway, I did something stupid. I needed three hundred bucks, you know, to get that necklace for Korie. I was gonna go in there and ask Mr. Miller to borrow the money 'cause he'd do anything for me. Then I come in, and he's sleepin' in front of the TV, and there's his wallet. And I take the money and just cut out of there. I'm figurin' on payin' it all back. I swear it, Coop."

"Oh man," Cooper said, "the old dude found out?"

"Worse, Coop. It's way worse than that. I take the money and go get the necklace. I'm thinkin' everything is cool. Next day I'm comin' home from school, and I meet Tuttle, this old devil who's the janitor in my building. He's tellin' me that Mr. Miller is dead." Roylin spoke heavily, the effort of each word like lifting wet cement.

"Dead?" Cooper repeated. "Dead from what?"

"He was pretty old, Coop. Tuttle said he saw me steal the money. He says Mr. Miller found his money gone from his wallet and started freakin' out. Tuttle said he was so upset when the money was gone that he got a heart attack and died of shock, all 'cause I stole the money. Tuttle says that makes me guilty of killin' Mr. Miller."

"What?!" Cooper cried.

"Yeah, Tuttle says that's the law. If you're robbin' someone and they die, then it's the same as if you shot them or something. You can get nailed for murder. Tuttle says I'm looking at life in prison. He saw the whole thing, and he even kept Mr. Miller's wallet with my fingerprints on it so he can prove I did it if I cross him."

"Roylin, lemme get this straight. This Miller dude died, and the cops came, right? So what did you tell them?" Cooper asked.

"No, no, see, Tuttle wrapped the body in a blanket and made me help him take it downstairs to the basement where he lives. And he's been digging this grave down there to bury Mr. Miller. And Tuttle says we gotta pretend he just moved away. Now that old devil is driving me like a servant and makin' me do all his chores, and he says if I don't keep on doing it, he's gonna turn me in to the cops, and that's the end of me," Roylin explained.

Cooper clasped his hands to the sides of his head and said, "Man, you really got yourself in a mess of trouble, Roylin. But listen up. How you so sure this old dude died of a heart attack? Maybe Tuttle seen you steal the money, and he got an idea. Tuttle goes in there and hits the old dude over the head or shoots him. Maybe Tuttle killed him his own self and plotted to blame you to get himself a servant. So, man, what did the body look like? You see any blood or bruises?"

"I never saw the body, Coop. By the time I got there, he'd wrapped Mr. Miller in blankets and put ropes around the body." Roylin winced at the horrible memory of carrying his old friend down to the basement.

"Listen to what I'm saying, Roylin. That old man's body could show that he was killed by some violent act. That would put you in the clear. Then you didn't make him die of a heart attack, okay?" Cooper explained.

Roylin stared at Cooper. "What am I gonna do? If I call the cops, they'll send me straight to jail. What if it *was* a heart attack? I'm in handcuffs in two seconds after Tuttle tells his story."

"Where did you say the man was buried?" Cooper asked.

"In the basement, next to the room where Tuttle lives. There's a stinking little corner there where Tuttle stores the garbage and stuff. The concrete is thin 'cause the place was dug up to fix some pipes. The workers just spread a little cement over it when they were done. So Tuttle, he broke it up, and that's where he put . . . Mr. Miller." Roylin said, barely getting out the words.

"Lemme see," Cooper said. "Does this Tuttle ever leave the building? Like is he ever gone long enough for us to do some lookin' into the matter?"

"Yeah, every Sunday he goes to the racetrack. He's gone all day, and he comes back late in the afternoon."

"Well, it's Sunday now." Cooper paused. Roylin looked at his watch. It was past 1:00 in the morning. "You got a way of getting down there?" he added.

"Yeah. But what are you getting at?" Roylin asked. Horror began to spread through his mind. "Cooper, what are you thinkin' of? You're not saying we should—"

"You got it," Cooper said. "We gotta dig the man up. We gotta see what killed the old dude as much as we can. That'll give us something to go on from there."

"I can't, Cooper . . . I just can't. I ain't got the stomach for it!" Roylin groaned.

"Roylin, listen up. I got a feelin' in my gut, you hear me? It was too smooth, too easy. Like this Tuttle sees you stealin', and all of a sudden the old dude wakes up and finds his cash missin'. He freaks and dies like that?" Cooper snapped his fingers. "Don't he go lookin' around like old people do, seein' if he put the money somewhere else? Don't it sound strange that he look in his wallet, and he's dead and cold in a few seconds? It just don't make sense."

"Yeah . . . you know, it does seem strange," Roylin admitted. He had not really thought about the details of what happened the day Mr. Miller died.

"Another thing," Cooper said, "if Mr. Miller was havin' a heart attack, how come Tuttle didn't call 911? That's what people do when somebody is havin' a heart attack. They don't just sit there and decide the dude is dead and ready for burial."

Roylin thought about what Cooper said. Maybe he was right. The possibility that something else might have caused Mr. Miller's death filled Roylin with a tangled knot of emotions. On one hand, he felt hope—hope that maybe he was not the reason his friend had a heart attack. On the other hand, he had still betrayed Mr. Miller, and his old friend was still gone forever. But what bothered him even more was that now he was not sure what really had happened. Maybe his death was not caused by a heart attack at all. Perhaps what happened was much worse. "You really think that old devil Tuttle might've killed Mr. Miller?" Roylin asked.

"Maybe. That's why we gotta see what we're dealin' with, Roylin. We gotta dig him up," Cooper said.

"Coop, there's no way I can do that," Roylin groaned.

"You *have* to!" he insisted. "And whatever happens, we gotta go to the cops."

"Cooper, we can't!"

"Easy now. I got an uncle who's a cop. He's a good guy, Roylin. He works with kids all the time. He knows when somebody's worth savin'. You got no rap sheet, right? I'll bring my uncle around, and he gonna work with you. You never meant nothin' but borrowin' some money from a friend. That ain't no serious crime. I'm swearin' to you, Roylin, I'm gonna be with you all through this, and you gonna come out all right."

"Coop, this ain't your problem. How come you're doin' all this for a punk like me?" Roylin asked.

"Don't be puttin' yourself down. You ain't no punk. No friend of Cooper Hodden's is a punk, you hear what I'm sayin'? We both in this together, man. Brothers, right?" Cooper clasped Roylin's hand. "Listen, Roylin. I know where you comin' from. Not everybody understands what it's like to have to watch your momma run from your dad 'cause he's beatin' her. But I do. I can't walk away from a brother who needs me. We gotta stick together and help each other. That's what this is all about. We're friends. Hear me?"

"Yeah, Coop, but I don't deserve a

friend like you," Roylin said. "I ain't been nobody's friend."

"Roylin, you were Mr. Miller's friend," Cooper reminded him.

"Yeah, right, and then I robbed him," Roylin said.

"You want me to smack you upside your head? You didn't mean to rob nobody. And you did him plenty good turns, didn't you?" Cooper demanded.

"Yeah. I'd get him stuff for his birthdays. One time I got him a nice sweater from the thrift store. He really liked that. He wore it all the time. Tuttle never turns up the heat in the apartments the way it should be, and Mr. Miller was always cold. He told me once that sweater was the nicest gift he ever got. Oh my God, Coop, I hope he wasn't wearin' that sweater when he died. I think he maybe had it on the last time I saw him. What if Tuttle buried him in it?"

Cooper grabbed Roylin by his shoulders and shook him. "Take it easy, man. You probably gave that old dude more joy than he ever got from anybody else. Whatever happened, you meant him no harm, you hear what I'm saying?"

Roylin tried to listen to Cooper's advice. But in his mind, all he could think about was finding his old friend's body in that cardigan sweater.

It was well past 2:00 a.m. when Roylin finally made it home. He and Cooper had agreed to meet again around noon. Even though he was exhausted, Roylin was unable to sleep. Just after sunrise, he heard his mother washing dishes in the kitchen. On weekends, she liked to get up early to have her "quiet time," as she called it. He did not want to talk to her or anyone, so he stayed in his bedroom. There was just too much on his mind, and he was not about to tell her that he planned to spend the afternoon digging up Mr. Miller in the basement. Just thinking about what he was going to do made shivers race through his body.

After a few hours, he heard Amber-lynn and the younger children getting dressed up and ready for church. Then he heard his mother walk up to his door. "Roylin, it wouldn't hurt you a bit to come to church, you know," she said.

"I will, Mom, next time," Roylin promised.

"Yeah, sure. You all the time sayin' that, and it never happens. You watch yourself. Pretty soon the Lord gonna get tired of waitin' on you!"

As soon as everybody left, Roylin washed and got dressed. Cooper showed up just as he finished. Cooper usually had a pleasant look on his face and a twinkle in his eye, but now he looked grim. "I got the shovels and a flashlight," Cooper said. "Let's go."

"I'm not sure I can go through with this," Roylin said. He felt sick to his stomach. His head was pounding.

"You can. Just think of something else while we work, Roylin," Cooper said in a flat voice.

They stepped carefully onto the rickety stairs and crept quietly into the dark room below. Roylin led the way through the debris-filled basement to the corner where the grave was. Gray metal garbage cans stood like tombstones in the basement's dim electric light. *This is no place for anyone to be buried,* Roylin thought, *let alone a good man like Mr. Miller.*

"Here, see where the dirt is freshly turned," Roylin whispered.

"Yeah, I see," Cooper said somberly. He grasped one of the shovels and handed the other to Roylin.

Roylin thought he was going to pass

out, but Cooper grabbed his shoulder and said, "Come on. We gotta do it."

Cooper turned over a spadeful of dirt, and then Roylin did the same. The freshly turned dirt was as soft as flour. Quickly, dirt began to pile up alongside the grave, and then Cooper's shovel hit something soft. "He didn't put him down very deep. I'm hitting something already, and we only went down about a foot," Cooper said.

Roylin was so sick to his stomach he thought he would vomit. But it was not from any smell coming from the grave. It was his own emotions churning up inside him. Fighting off the nausea, Roylin dug a little more. Then both boys dropped to their knees and began scooping soil away with their bare hands.

Roylin recognized the dull gray blanket as the one that had been on Mr. Miller's bed for years. The rope was still wrapped around the body. Tears filled Roylin's eyes, blurring the sight before him as they scooped and brushed the dirt from the blanket until the length of the body was exposed in its shallow grave.

Cooper pulled out a knife and cut the twine. "We gonna cut through the blanket and have a look," Cooper said grimly.

"No need takin' the body out of the grave right now. We just gonna see what we're dealin' with, and then we gonna call my uncle."

"Oh my God, oh my God," Roylin moaned.

"Take it easy, man. Gonna be better when Mr. Miller is taken away and given a decent burial. He don't belong in a place like this. It's disrespectful," Cooper said. "Here we go now." He started cutting through the blanket to get to what was underneath. "Hang on . . . I'm almost getting through now." Cooper gently peeled back the blanket.

Roylin forced himself to stare down into the grave. He expected to see the red and white cardigan sweater, but all he saw was dull gray burlap.

"Look like he wrapped in something else too," Cooper said. He slashed carefully at the burlap, and then he gasped, "We onto something big here!"

There was a small light hanging overhead on the other side of the basement, but it was not enough to see clearly into the grave. Roylin grabbed the flashlight Cooper had put down and shined it into the shallow hole. He gasped at what he saw.

Chapter 10

"Where is he?" Roylin asked in an anguished voice. "Where's Mr. Miller?"

Cooper reached down into the pit with both hands and came up with nothing but sandbags and sand. Amazement and relief swept through Roylin Bailey. Mr. Miller was not buried in the basement after all. But where *was* he? Maybe he was not dead—maybe he was alive somewhere! "Oh man, and all this time I thought poor Mr. Miller was buried in this stinkin' place!" Roylin shouted.

"Look like Tuttle wrapped the blanket around the sand bags to make it look and feel like a body," Cooper said, "But where's the old dude then?"

"You think Tuttle buried him somewhere else?" Roylin asked, dread returning to his heart.

Cooper shrugged. "Only one way to find out. When old Tuttle comes home this afternoon, we meet him right here. We surprise him by standing by this pit here, and maybe we gonna shock him so much he tells the truth."

"Cooper, I'll never forget what you've done for me, standin' by me like this," Roylin said.

"It ain't over yet," Cooper said. He looked at his watch. "Tuttle gonna be back in a coupla hours. I'm starvin'. We got time to grab some burgers and get back here."

The boys drove to a nearby fast food restaurant and got burgers and fries. For the first time in two weeks, Roylin enjoyed a meal. He at least had the hope now that he had not caused his friend's death, that Mr. Miller had not died after all.

After eating, Roylin and Cooper went back to the apartment building and waited by the open grave. Tuttle was very predictable. He always came and went at the same times. Today was no different. At a few minutes after 5:00, the sounds of Tuttle's off-key whistling echoed upstairs. He seemed in good humor. He must have been lucky at the racetrack today. He walked slowly down the stairs into the basement. Then, at the bottom, he flicked on the light.

"Lemme handle this," Cooper whispered moments before Tuttle made his appearance. Roylin did not mind. Cooper was about six inches taller than he was. On the football field, Cooper intimidated Bluford's opponents just by looking at them. Since he shaved his head, he looked even scarier.

Now Cooper darted into Tuttle's path, casting a huge shadow over the little man. "Hey, Tuttle, me and Roylin dug up Mr. Miller's grave, and we know what went down. We know the whole story, and now we want to hear what you got to say for yourself, or else maybe you want to use that grave for your own self."

Roylin knew the little man was instantly terrified. Tuttle backed away from Cooper, his mouth twitching violently, his red-rimmed eyes wide with fear. "What? What are you talkin' about?"

Cooper backed Tuttle into a corner and barked into his trembling face. "Just say what happened, man, and you better not forget anything 'cause I'm about to blow up, Tuttle. When I get mad I don't leave nothin' standin'."

Tuttle's mouth formed itself into a sick, desperate smile. "It was just a little joke. Just a little joke is all. Nobody got hurt. I saw Roylin take the old man's money, and I thought the boy needed to be taught a lesson. Yeah, that was it. I was only tryin' to help the boy. And see, it was time for the demented old man to be sent away anyway, so I just hurried it up a little."

Roylin's legs felt weak. Had Tuttle killed Mr. Miller?

Tuttle was now standing at the edge of the grave. He stared down at it nervously from time to time. "I just sent the old man away to a nursing home and played this little joke."

"Nursing home?! Joke?!!" Roylin managed to cry out, his mouth trembling and his eyes filling with tears. Mr. Miller was still alive!

"That ain't no joke, Tuttle," said Cooper. "That's sick. You were just lookin' for someone to do your work for you!"

Cooper moved closer to Tuttle, and the little man lost his balance, tumbling into the shallow grave. He cowered there in the dirt, the whites of his eyes glowing in the murky darkness. "Don't hurt me," he wept. "Please, don't hurt me. No harm was done, no harm."

"You made me think I caused the death of somebody I cared about," Roylin cried. "I didn't want to live anymore 'cause of you. I was thinkin' about killin' myself!" Roylin trembled as he spoke.

"Where's Mr. Miller, Tuttle?" Cooper demanded.

"One of those nursing homes," Tuttle stammered. "Please, look, I'll give you money. How much you want? I'll pay you if you don't hurt me." Tuttle groped in his pockets for what looked like a couple of hundred dollars. He held it towards Roylin and Cooper.

Cooper took the money and then let all the bills flutter back into Tuttle's face as he sat in the shallow grave. "You like some demon out of hell," Cooper said, shaking his head. "You belong down here with the garbage." As he talked, Cooper picked up his shovel and took a step towards Tuttle, towering over the little man. "Now, tell me *exactly* where Mr. Miller is, or you might not walk out of this basement," Cooper growled.

"Cottonwood Court," Tuttle whined. "Please, let me go."

"What d'ya think, Roylin? Seem a shame to let that nice grave go to waste," Cooper said in his most sinister voice.

"Yeah, I hate for stuff to go to waste," Roylin agreed.

"Please, no, please," Tuttle whimpered.

Cooper and Roylin turned and silently walked up the stairs and out the door.

"Coop," Roylin said, "I feel like a ton of bricks just fell off my chest. I feel like *I* was the one just crawled out of a grave. I don't ever want to feel like that again."

Cooper grinned at last, looking like himself again. "Likely that good-for-nothin' ain't gonna be playin' tricks like that again on anybody. He's so scared, I think the last tooth in his mouth got rattled out from shakin'."

"Coop, you're the best friend a guy ever had. Man, I'll always remember this. Listen to me. If you ever need a friend, I'll be there for you. I don't care what time of the day or night, I'll be there. I mean it, Coop. You're the best there is!"

Cooper grinned and playfully punched Roylin in the chest. "Gotta go now. Tarah wants me to take her to this stupid movie where everybody sits around and talks. It's real boring. No fights, no car chases, nothin' but some fool whisperin' to his girl about how much he loves her. Maybe I can get some sleep in the movie if those fools in the picture ain't whining or cryin' too loud."

When Roylin finally returned to his apartment, his mother was fixing dinner, and Amberlynn was cutting up vegetables. "You want me to help with anything?" Roylin asked.

Roylin's mother looked at Amberlynn and then at Roylin. "You got a fever, boy?" his mother asked.

Roylin smiled. He remembered the words of an old hymn he heard in church. He could not remember the words exactly, but he recalled enough to say, "Mom, I was dead and now I'm alive . . . I was blind and now I see."

Mom smiled. "Well, see your way over to that cabinet and take out the dishes and set the table."

His mother's smile warmed Roylin's heart like it never had before. He would do right by her now. He would do right by everyone.

Chapter 11

At lunchtime on Monday, Roylin called the Cottonwood Court Nursing Home. "You got a man there. His name is Ambrose Miller, and I want to know if I can visit him, 'cause he's my friend," Roylin said.

"You can visit any time during the day," a woman with a pleasant voice said.

"We go back a long way," Roylin explained. "Listen, I was thinkin'. Could I take Mr. Miller out to lunch on week-ends and stuff like that? 'Cause we like to go for cheeseburgers once in a while."

"That would be fine. You can come any day you want. Our guests are always happy for outings. Just be sure to bring some identification with you. It's the rule. We have our own little trips for guests, but it means so much more if a friend or a loved one comes," the woman said.

For so many days and nights, Roylin had been haunted by the guilt of contributing to Mr. Miller's death. Now he had a second chance. He had feared the worst and come through with the help of one good friend—Cooper Hodden. Now Roylin felt strangely light, as if he could float from class to class and be friends with everybody if he wanted, even those who would not return the friendship. He could even forgive Korie Archer.

At school that afternoon, Roylin was able to look at Korie Archer and smile and say, "How's it goin'?" Korie looked confused. She did not say a word.

When Roylin ran into Steve, he smiled at him too, stuck out his hand, and said, "No hard feelings, right?"

Steve stared at Roylin for a minute as if he expected some trick. Then he held out his hand and said, "Right."

"Sorry I lost it the other day," Roylin said. "I was goin' through a rough time."

"Forget about it," Steve said.

Immediately after school, Roylin drove up to Cottonwood Court. As he pulled into the parking lot, he saw little sign of life, but the grounds were green and neat. The quiet, tidy beauty reminded Roylin of a cemetery. Inside, the place was nothing luxurious, but it was clean and pleasant, with warm ivory walls and green linoleum. Many elderly people moved slowly in wheelchairs or walkers. The admitting nurse told Roylin that Mr. Miller had no guests since he had arrived, except for the lawyer his daughter designated to handle his affairs.

"Where is Mr. Miller now?" Roylin asked. Frail, elderly people moved by with painful slowness, but that was not the saddest part of it. They seemed to be looking around for familiar faces, and there were none, except for the nurses.

"He's in his room," the nurse said. "Our guests live two to a room. Mr. Miller does not like to mix with the other guests. He hasn't been to the activity room. Are you his grandson?"

"I'm sorta that, yeah," Roylin said. Mr. Miller had two grandsons living back East. They were in some nice college somewhere. Mr. Miller had not seen them in years.

Roylin passed the activity room where a young woman was reading a story. Nobody seemed to be listening. Most of the old people looked like they were sleeping. Two elderly men were

116

playing cards, and one lady was knitting.

And then Roylin saw Mr. Miller. There was a television set blaring in the room, but Mr. Miller wasn't watching it. He sat in a chair dozing, his chin resting on his chest. He was wearing the red and white sweater Roylin had given him.

"Hello, Mr. Miller," Roylin said softly, even though his heart was racing.

Mr. Miller's head jerked up. He looked around in confusion. "Is my daughter here?" he asked. "Is Jenny here?"

The nurse who was with Roylin said, "I'm sorry, Mr. Miller, your daughter isn't here, but you have a visitor."

Tears filled Roylin's eyes as Mr. Miller looked up and seemed to show no sign of recognition. Roylin dropped to his knees beside Mr. Miller's chair. "It's me, Roylin," he said anxiously.

"Roylin?" Mr. Miller said, his mouth twitching with the trace of a smile. "Is that you, boy?" He fumbled for his glasses and put them on. "It *is* you. Where you been, boy?"

"I came as soon as I heard you were here, Mr. Miller," Roylin answered.

"I don't know why I'm here, Roylin. I was paying my rent. What did they bring me here for? It's like I done something wrong. I didn't do nothing wrong." He looked all around the small room, "I don't even know where I am."

"You're in Cottonwood Court. It's a nursing home. How is it living here, Mr. Miller?" Roylin asked.

"I don't rightly know. The food is okay, but it's like bein' in jail, Roylin. They talk to you like you're some fool kid. And my little cars are gone. I ain't seen my little cars since I come here."

"Tuttle took them, but I'll try to get them back," Roylin said.

"Did Jenny come by? I didn't see her. Why don't she come, Roylin? She don't care if I live or die, and I'm her father. I'm her father, boy." Tears rolled down the old man's craggy face. "My God, a girl should give a care for her own father."

"I'm sorry, Mr. Miller," Roylin said.

"I won't never get out of here, will I, boy? This is like some waiting room in a funeral home. I won't never see the lights of the neighborhood again."

"Maybe you will, Mr. Miller," said Roylin, turning to the nurse. "I'd like to take Mr. Miller out for a drive. You can see it'd mean a lot to him."

The nurse looked at Roylin's school ID, and then said, "This young man would like to take you out, Mr. Miller. Would you like to go out with him?"

"If I don't, I may go crazy," Mr. Miller mumbled.

Turning to Roylin, the nurse said softly, "This may be just what he needs. He's been very depressed. If an outing will do him any good, it would be good news to the whole staff. Just be sure and bring him back by 7:00."

"Great," said Roylin. "Come on, Mr. Miller, we can get out of here for a while."

"Could we get some real food, boy? The food here is mushy. Lord, I got teeth yet. What I'd do for one of those cheeseburgers you and me used to have. You think we could get some of them?"

Mr. Miller used a cane just in case he had a dizzy spell, but he could walk without any support. He walked beside Roylin out of the facility and into the parking lot. Roylin held open the door as Mr. Miller got into the Honda. Then they drove towards town.

"My . . . look at all the folks walkin' around," Mr. Miller said. "Busy, busy. I used to be like that. Wasn't enough time in the day to do all I had to do. Now I got nothin' to do and plenty of time to do it. I used to carry the mail, you know. I told you that. Had my wife, my Amelia, sweetest little woman a man ever had. My little girl, Jenny. She was Daddy's little girl. Used to run and throw her arms around me when I got home from work. I worked in the yard, had vegetables, fruit trees. It was a good life, Roylin. It seems only yesterday . . . I was such a lucky man."

They pulled into the hamburger drive-thru and ordered two jumbo cheeseburgers.

Roylin thought about confessing to Mr. Miller that he had taken the two hundred and fifty dollars, but he figured that would only hurt Mr. Miller. Instead, Roylin would pay him back—and more—in cheeseburgers and gifts. They would hang out together, and he would buy his old friend more warm cardigan sweaters and new toy cars. He would try to make Mr. Miller as happy as Mr. Miller had made him when he was a little boy. Once Mr. Miller was his only ray of sunshine, and now he would be Mr. Miller's escape from the waiting room of the funeral home.

After Roylin brought Mr. Miller back to Cottonwood Court, he went home and confronted Tuttle. "What did you do with Mr. Miller's little cars?" Roylin demanded. "He wants them back."

Tuttle looked frightened. He had all the little cars in cartons waiting to be sold at a collector's show. Now he scurried to his room and brought the cartons, giving them all to Roylin. "Here's the cars. I didn't take none of them. What's an old man want with them anyway?" Tuttle asked.

Roylin grabbed the cartons. "We like to look at them together and remember the old days. And don't you call my friend an old man, Tuttle. And, listen up, you get hot water going in the apartments, or I'm calling the Health Department, you hear me?"

After history class on Tuesday, a group of students—Hakeem, Darcy, Cooper, Tarah, Brisana, and others—were talking in the hall about the grades they got on their reports. Roylin felt all of these students were winners. They each had something wonderful, like brains, personality, beauty, athletic skill, whatever. Roylin figured he never had any of these things, so he always felt uncomfortable around such people. His usual response was to taunt others to make himself feel better. But now Roylin swallowed his nervousness and walked into the middle of the group. "You guys," he said, "listen up. I got a great idea."

"A great idea, Roylin?" Darcy asked. "Does this mean you have someone new to torture?"

"No, no," Roylin said. "I got this friend, Ambrose Miller, a really nice old guy, and he's out at this nursing home—it's called Cottonwood Court. There are lots of old people there, and nobody much visits them, not even their families most of the time. I figure we could maybe go see them once in a while, bring cookies, stuff like that."

There was a long silence until Brisana said, "Yeah, right. What a great idea. We can spend all our free time with a bunch of old people." She began to laugh at her own comment, but nobody joined in her laughter.

"Sounds like a great idea to me," Cooper said.

"I could play my guitar. It'd be fun," Hakeem said.

"Instead of spendin' our time shoving pizza into our faces, we could do somethin' really good. You guys, this is a really nice idea. Let's do it," Tarah said.

Roylin looked around, surprised that his idea had gone over so well. Just weeks ago, he would never have believed that something he had to say would be considered worthwhile. He was still Roylin Bailey, C-minus student, mediocre football player with average looks, slouching shoulders, and the not-so-great personality—but the other kids were looking at him with respect now.

On Saturday, about a dozen students from Bluford went to Cottonwood Court for an afternoon visit. Some of the usually listless old people clapped and sang when Hakeem played some older tunes on his guitar. Roylin took Mr. Miller out afterwards for a drive through the neighborhood to see the sights he loved so much.

"You're my best friend, Mr. Miller," he said, suddenly finding himself overcome with emotion.

Mr. Miller smiled brightly, his eyes twinkling in the light. "You're my best friend too, boy. Always been. Always been."

On Monday, Roylin was eating lunch with Cooper and Tarah when Korie came over.

"Hi, Roylin," she said, looking around nervously. "Can we talk?"

"Sure," he replied. Slowly he stood up, and they walked over to an empty table nearby.

"Roylin, I'm sorry about everything."

"Stuff happens," Roylin said.

"I really do like you. I liked you from the first day. I mean, you must think I was nice to you just to get the necklace, but I liked you, too," Korie said.

Roylin stopped walking and turned to Korie. He looked at her satin black hair, her lovely face, the dark eyes with lashes that went on forever. She was still the most beautiful creature Roylin had ever seen.

"Steve's okay, but he's not as nice as you, Roylin," Korie said. "He's so full of himself, you know what I mean?" Korie reached over and grasped Roylin's hand. Her warm soft fingers wrapped around his. "Roylin, I know Steve is a running back with the Buccaneers, but I like a person who's nice and sincere. I wish it could be like it was before with you and me."

"You're really something, Korie," Roylin said. "I sure wanted to be with you. What guy wouldn't?"

"We can go out together again then, can't we? I mean, it's not working with me and Steve."

Roylin looked right into Korie's eyes. A few weeks ago he would have done anything to hear her say what she just said. But now Roylin felt like he was looking at a beautiful statue. Roylin did not quite know why she wanted to come back to him. Maybe Steve did not want to buy Korie nice things. Maybe she liked Roylin now because a lot of other people liked him better. Or maybe she was sincere, and something about Roylin just attracted her. Today Roylin was willing to believe that was possible.

But Cooper Hodden's words came back to Roylin: *"I wouldn't take six Korie Archers for one Tarah Carson . . . she got heart."*

Roylin Bailey had gone through hell these past few weeks. The flames had singed his soul, but now he had come out on the other side. He did not hate himself anymore. He did not need to tear somebody else down to feel big. He did not need a pretty girl on his arm to feel good.

"Korie, you're a beautiful girl," Roylin said slowly, "but not for me . . . not for me no more."

Korie seemed shocked as Roylin walked on alone. Roylin was already thinking ahead. He would bring the little cars out to Cottonwood Court on Saturday morning, and he and Mr. Miller would look at them again. Then, they'd go for burgers. On Sunday, Roylin would hang out with Hakeem and Darcy, Cooper and Tarah, and some other kids he was getting to know.

For the first time in his life, Roylin Bailey believed he was on earth for a purpose. For the first time in his life, it felt good to be Roylin Bailey.

Find out what happens next at

BLUFORD HIGH

Someone to Love Me

At first, Bobby Wallace was everything Cindy Gibson hoped for. He was friendly, seemingly mature, and handsome—the perfect escape from her problems in school and even bigger troubles at home. But then, Bobby starts behaving strangely, and Cindy gets scared. Hiding her concerns from her friends and her distracted mother, Cindy soon finds herself in the worst trouble of her life.

Turn the page for a special sneak preview. . . .

The doorbell rang. "Who is it?" Cindy cried, walking towards the door.

"It's me. Open up," a familiar voice said.

Cindy opened the door to find Jamee Wills, another Bluford freshman, staring at her.

"Cindy!" Jamee shouted. "Girl, what're you doing in pajamas? It's time to go to school."

"I'm not going to school," Cindy said firmly. "Why don't you cut too? We can watch TV, and I got popcorn we can stick in the microwave. And there's pizza in the freezer, too. Today on Paula Poole's show—"

"Cindy! Girl, get it together!" Jamee said, stepping into the apartment. "You need to throw on some clothes and come to school. Keep this up, you gonna be so far behind that you can't do nothin' but fail."

"You don't understand—" Cindy replied, looking down at the worn flip-flops on her feet.

"I understand all right. I understand you gotta get back on track," Jamee replied. "Remember in middle school, Mr. Schuman said you were such a good artist you could be a famous cartoonist for Disney or something? How you gonna be famous if you don't go to school?"

Cindy shrugged. "I can't hang around school all day, Jamee. I get bored. Who cares anyway? My mom wouldn't mind if I quit school. We all just wasting our time in school anyway. Ain't none of us goin' anywhere."

"Cindy, you're crazy," Jamee said, tugging on Cindy's arm. "My sister, Darcy, she's already planning to go to college, and so is her friend Tarah. I'm gonna do the same thing, and you can do it too. But first you gotta get up, change them clothes and get to school. Now come on!"

"Just leave me alone," Cindy insisted.

"Cindy, please come to school."

"Jamee, cut school with me today," Cindy moaned. "If you don't wanna watch TV, I got some CD's we could play and—"

"I'm outta here," Jamee snapped. "I'm not gonna sit here and watch you throw your life away!" Jamee stormed towards the doorway. "When you want to do something with yourself besides sit here watching TV, call me," she said, walking out the door and slamming it behind her. The loud crash of the door was followed by a heavy silence.

Cindy moved to the window and watched Jamee shift her backpack and join the stream of kids heading for Bluford. Part of her wanted to join the crowd and head to school, but another part of her did not want to move. Unlike Jamee and her classmates, Cindy felt foreign and out of place at school. Her teachers often said she was "quiet" and "shy," but Cindy knew she was just different.

Turning from the window, Cindy grabbed the magazines on the living room floor and stacked them neatly on the coffee table. Then she picked up a pile of dirty clothes she had left sitting on the living room chair for weeks.

"Yuck, these stink!" Cindy groaned. It had been a while since she had washed her laundry. Sometimes she just picked an outfit from the dirty clothes pile to wear to school. As long as things were not too dirty or wrinkled, she would still wear them. It had not always been this way. In fact, Cindy did have a few new clothes that she got for the start of her freshman year. But as weeks passed and her mother spent less and less time at home, laundry, like school, seemed less important.

Glancing around the cluttered living room, Cindy focused on the small picture of her mother that sat next to the TV. Raffie, her mother's boyfriend, was also in the picture, his arm resting on her shoulder like a heavy snake. Only a few months old, the picture captured her mother's flawless milk-chocolate skin and her radiant smile. *Mom is beautiful,* Cindy thought, *and I look nothing like her.* Where her mother was tall, curvy, and attractive, Cindy was long and skinny. But worse than her lanky shape was her nose. To Cindy, it seemed to spread too far across the middle of her face, making her feel that her head was just a platform on which her nose rested.

Friends of her mother had always been kind, but even they noticed how different Cindy was. *"Oh, I can't see a resemblance,"* they would politely begin. *"You must take after your father."* Cindy knew exactly what they were trying to say, but she appreciated their attempt to spare her feelings.

The only person who did not seem concerned with Cindy's feelings was Raffie. *"Are you sure she's your momma?"* he asked Cindy when he began dating her mother last year. When Cindy first met him, he was sitting at the kitchen table, gold chains jangling around his neck, gold earrings glittering from his earlobes, and a smirk on his face.

"You ain't nothin' like your momma," he had said. *"She is what a man would call one hot lady."* Since then, Cindy did her best to ignore Raffie, but it was not easy. Often he said things that made her feel even worse about her looks, but he always did it out of Mom's earshot, calling Cindy "Ugly Mugly" and flaring his nostrils to taunt her. Whenever Cindy asked him to stop, he would laugh in her face. Once, he even flapped his arms in a mock imitation of her long, awkward limbs.

In August, Cindy's mother announced that she and Raffie were "serious," and since then, she spent most of her free time with him. In the rare moments Mom was home, all she could talk about was Raffie. Cindy cringed each time she heard his name. It seemed to her that Raffie was gradually taking over her mother's life. Worse, it appeared as if that was exactly what Mom wanted.

Alone in the apartment, Cindy sat in the recliner in front of the TV and turned it on with the remote control. She had to push hard to make the recliner go back into a comfortable position. The old chair did not work as well as it used to, and Mom said she did not make enough money at her waitressing job to buy a new one.

Cindy had believed her until she noticed her mother frequently buying herself new outfits to wear for Raffie. It seemed that once a week Mom came home carrying shopping bags from expensive department stores. When Cindy asked her about it, Mom explained that Raffie had been giving her money so she could buy nice clothes, but this only made Cindy more upset. It was as if Raffie was buying her mother away from her, and there was nothing Cindy could do to stop it.

Cindy began flipping through the channels when she heard the doorbell ring. Annoyed, she turned toward the door and called out, "Yeah? Who is it?"

"Mrs. Davis, honey," came a familiar voice. Rose Davis lived at the other end of the hall. She was raising her fifteen-year-old grandson, Harold. Once, in the basement laundry room, Cindy overheard Mrs. Davis tell a neighbor that Harold's mother had died in childbirth, and his father never was in the picture.

Cindy got up and opened the door. "Hi, Mrs. Davis."

"Child, I heard the TV goin', so I figured you were home. I was worried about you. Ain't you supposed to be in school?" Mrs. Davis asked.

"Uh . . . I got cramps," Cindy lied, rubbing her hand on her stomach.

"Poor thing! I make tea that's real soothin' for that. I'll bring you some if you like," Mrs. Davis offered.

"No, thank you. I just took something. I'll feel better soon," Cindy said, smiling.

Rose Davis stared at her for a moment. Cindy braced herself for criticism about not being in school. But then the old woman began to smile. "Child, you got the prettiest eyes I ever did see," she said.

"Me?" Cindy said, stunned. "You must be thinkin' of my mom. She's got real pretty eyes with long lashes, but my eyes are—"

"I never noticed before that you got the prettiest hazel-brown eyes, Cindy," Mrs. Davis added. "Folks say the eyes are windows to the soul. They believe you can look someone right in the eye and tell what kind of person they are."

"Some boy in school says I have freak eyes," Cindy said. "Now, him and all his friends call me that whenever they see me."

Mrs. Davis grabbed hold of Cindy's shoulders and looked into her face. "Child, your eyes are beautiful, and don't you forget that. Pay no mind to what a boy says 'bout you. My grandson Harold tells me that some of them kids at your school can be downright nasty sometimes. It's like I tell him—when they start talkin' that nonsense, you just stop listenin'. Let 'em call you names. But it's you who's got the prettiest eyes around, not them. Remember that."

As she spoke, Mrs. Davis gently placed her hand on Cindy's cheek. "Some people need to see their own beauty before they can believe they got it," she said, smiling. Mrs. Davis waved goodbye and headed down the long hallway.

Cindy hurried to the bathroom mirror and stared into it. She stood for a long time, moving her face in close for a better look. Her mother had a mirror that magnified everything, and Cindy looked in that too. Her large hazel eyes stared back at her. *Did Mrs. Davis mean what she said, or was she being nice?* Cindy wondered.

Leaving the TV on, Cindy jumped in the shower and washed her hair. Then she gathered her dirty clothes, took them downstairs and put them in the washing machine. When the clothes were dry, she brought them back upstairs, folded them neatly and put them into her drawers. It was the first time she had done her laundry in weeks.

After putting the clothes away, Cindy found a pair of white jeans and two ribbed tank tops, one blue and the other green and yellow. *Maybe I'll go to school tomorrow wearing one of these tank tops*, she thought. Probably not, but if she felt like it in the morning, she might go. Mom would write a note explaining that she had been sick. Mom never seemed to care what excuses Cindy used to skip school. Cindy practically dictated them, always remembering to vary the made-up ailments. She used headaches until a nosy teacher started pushing her to see a doctor. Then she added cramps and fevers to her list of illnesses.

As Cindy thought about returning to school, she again recalled what Mrs. Davis said about her having "the prettiest eyes." She grabbed her mother's magnifying mirror and sat on the recliner looking into it. Cindy tried hard to see what Mrs. Davis saw.

"Maybe my eyes *are* pretty," Cindy said into the mirror.

On Paula Poole's show, two sisters who were married to the same man were screaming at each other. The show kept bleeping out the bad words flying between them, and when they started pulling each other's hair, the audience went wild. Everybody was laughing and cheering.

But Cindy did not pay much attention to the show. She kept staring in the mirror, trying out different expressions to see how they changed the look of her eyes. Maybe she wasn't that bad looking, she thought. With her hair clean and brushed, she didn't think she looked as ugly as Raffie said. And she had clearer skin than most of the other kids at school.

Suddenly the phone rang. Cindy put the mirror down and answered it.

"Hello," she said.

"Yo—who's this?" a familiar deep-throated voice replied.

"It's me," Cindy answered.

"Oh, Ugly Mugly," Raffie Whitaker said. "How come you home? You get suspended for messin' up at school again?"

"I never been suspended," Cindy corrected him sharply. "And stop calling me that."

Raffie laughed. He always chuckled when he upset Cindy. She could just imagine him on the other end of the line—smiling in satisfaction at how he managed to insult her. "C'mon, Ugly Mugly. Where's your momma?" he asked, still laughing.

"I told you to stop calling me that," Cindy demanded. She wished she could reach into the telephone and wrap the cord around his neck.

"Girl, you so ugly," Raffie went on, in between bursts of cackling laughter, "when the doctor delivered you, he was wearin' a blindfold."

Cindy slammed down the phone. in about a second it rang again. She turned up the TV volume to drown out the ringing. One of the sisters on the Paula Poole show had a nail file, and she looked as if she was about to attack the other one with it. Maybe it was all an act, but the hate in the girl's face seemed real. It was the same hatred Cindy felt for Raffie.

Cindy fantasized about being on the show with Raffie Whitaker. She imagined herself grabbing the gold chains he hung around his neck and pulling them so tight his eyes bulged out.

The phone kept ringing. "I ain't gonna answer you. You can't make me." Cindy smiled because for once she had power. Raffie Whitaker was fuming somewhere, and he could not do a thing about it.

Ignoring the phone's periodic ringing, Cindy picked up the mirror again and repeated the words that Mrs. Davis had said. "Pretty eyes . . . pretty hazel eyes."

Maybe Mrs. Davis was not the only one who thought she was special. Maybe someone else would feel that way about her too one day.